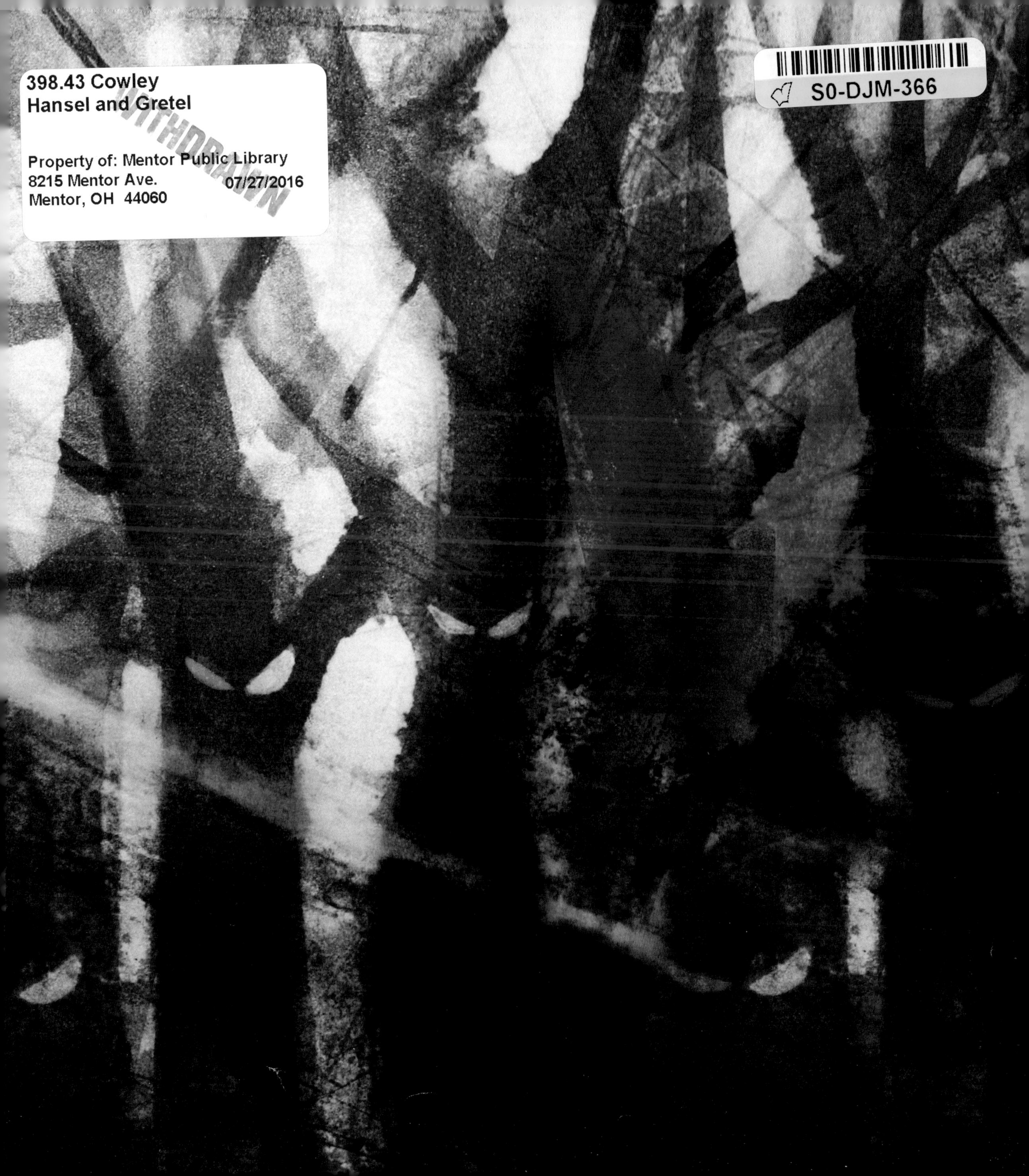

# big & SMALL

Original Korean text by Hee-jeong Yoon
Illustrations by Hyeon-sook Jo
Korean edition © Yeowon Media Co., Ltd.

This English edition published by big & SMALL in 2015
by arrangement with Yeowon Media Co., Ltd.
English text edited by Joy Cowley
English edition © big & SMALL 2015

Distributed in the United States and Canada by
Lerner Publishing Group, Inc.
241 First Avenue North
Minneapolis, MN 55401 U.S.A.
www.lernerbooks.com

ISBN: 978-1-925186-66-6

Printed in the United States of America
1 – CG – 5/31/15

# Hansel and Gretel

A story by the Brothers Grimm
retold by Joy Cowley
Illustrated by Hyeon-sook Jo

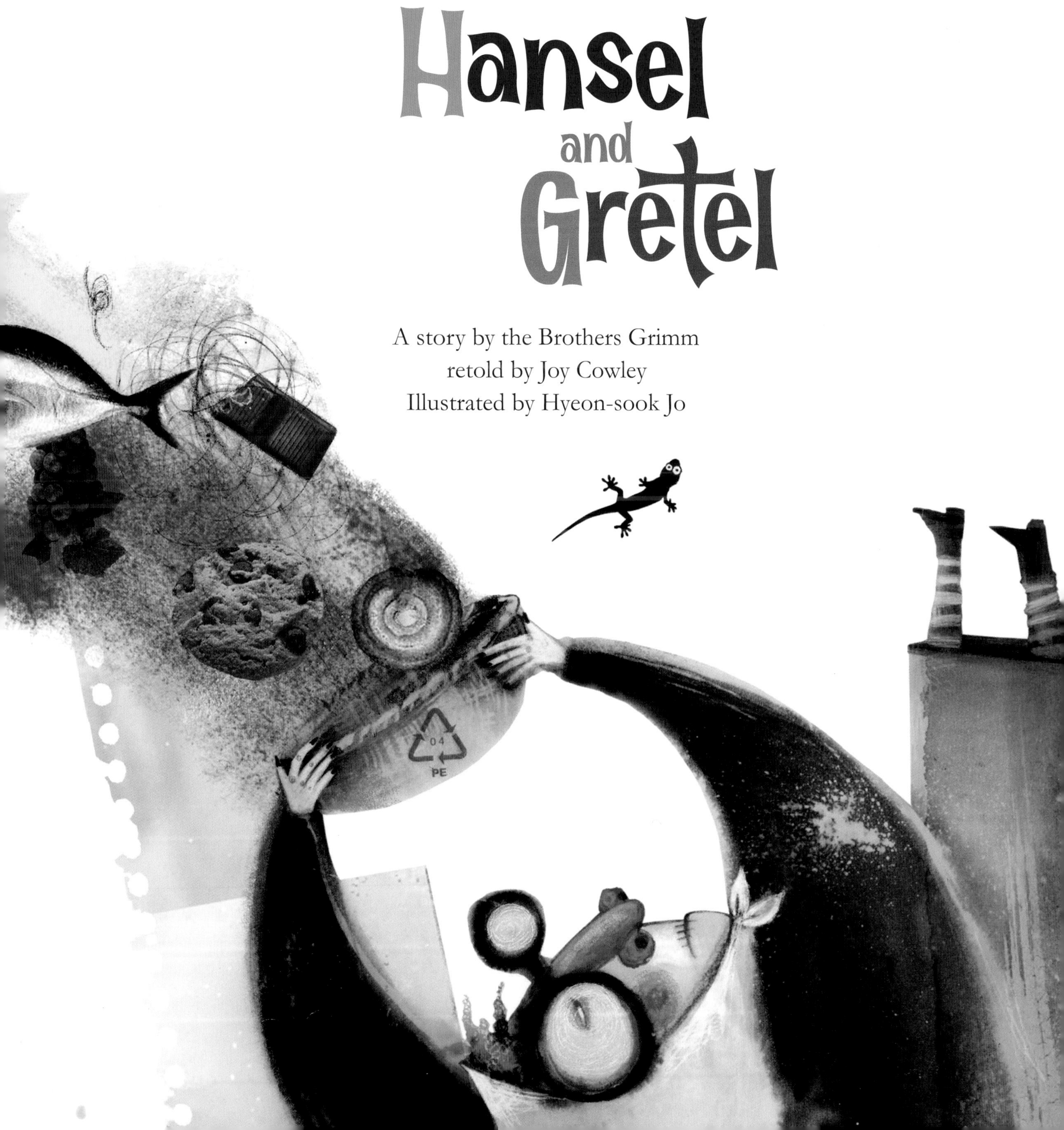
04
PE

In the forest lived the woodcutter, his wife and their two children, Hansel and Gretel. They were a happy family until the wife died and the woodcutter married again. Hansel and Gretel's stepmother did not like the children.

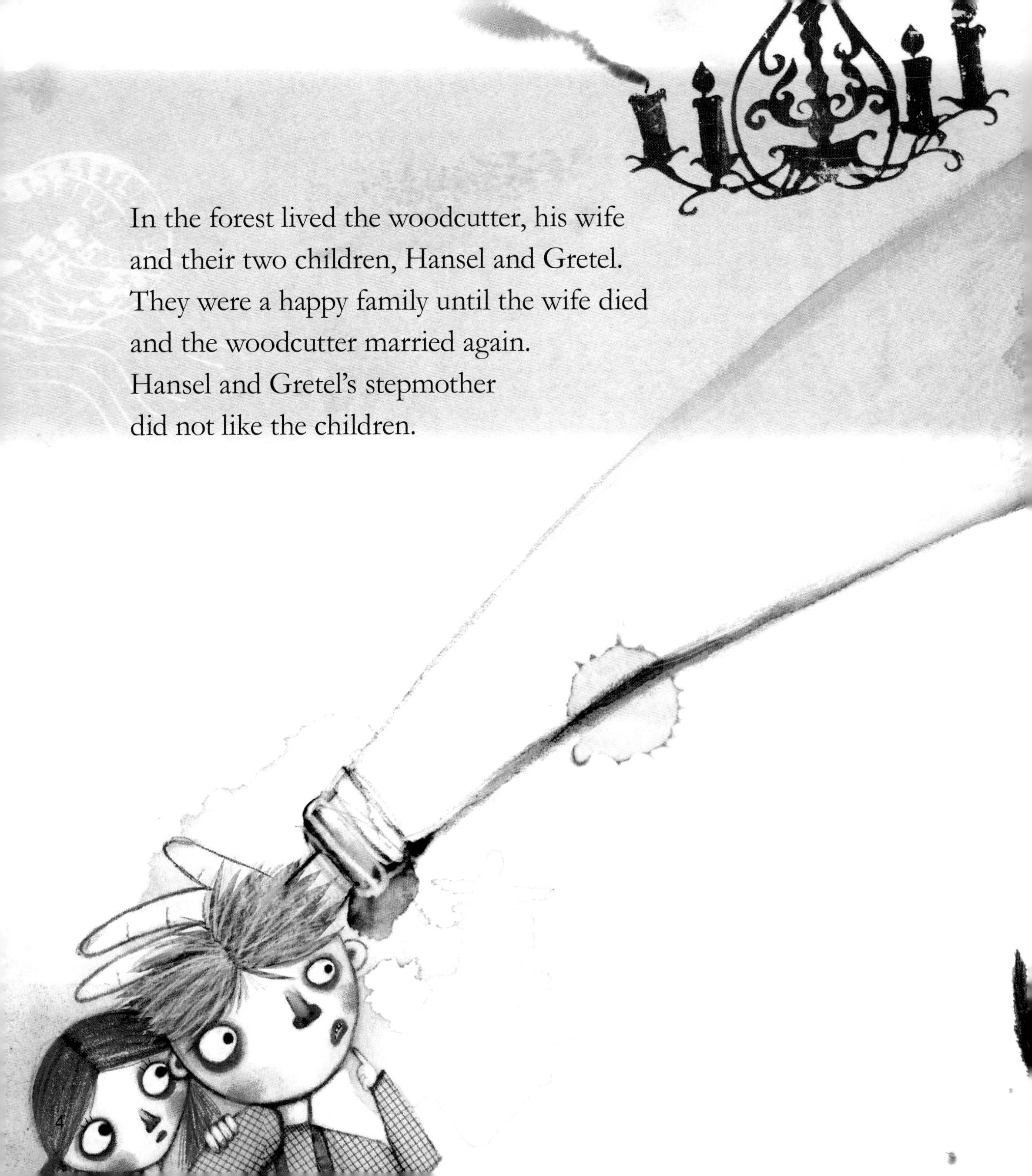

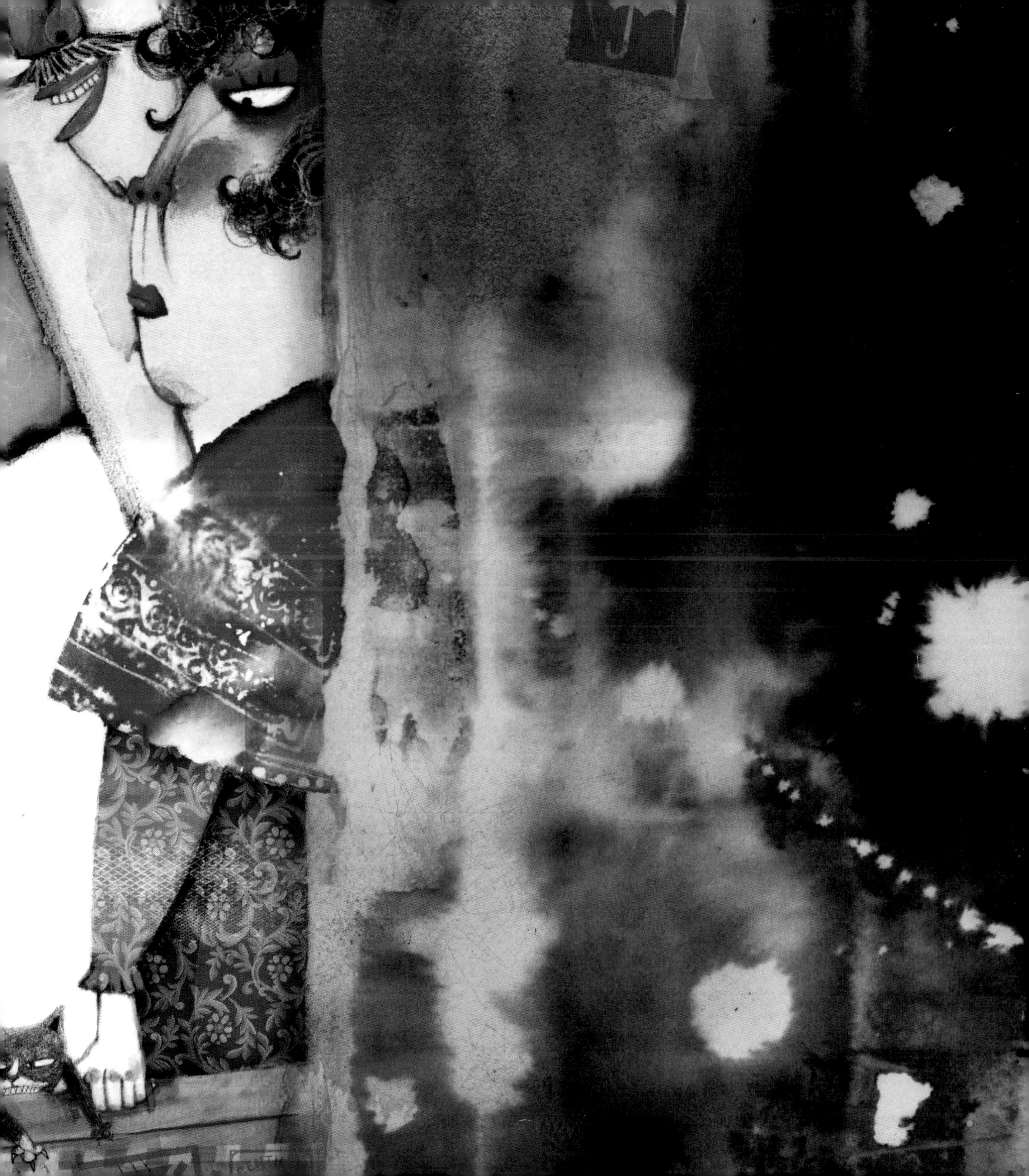

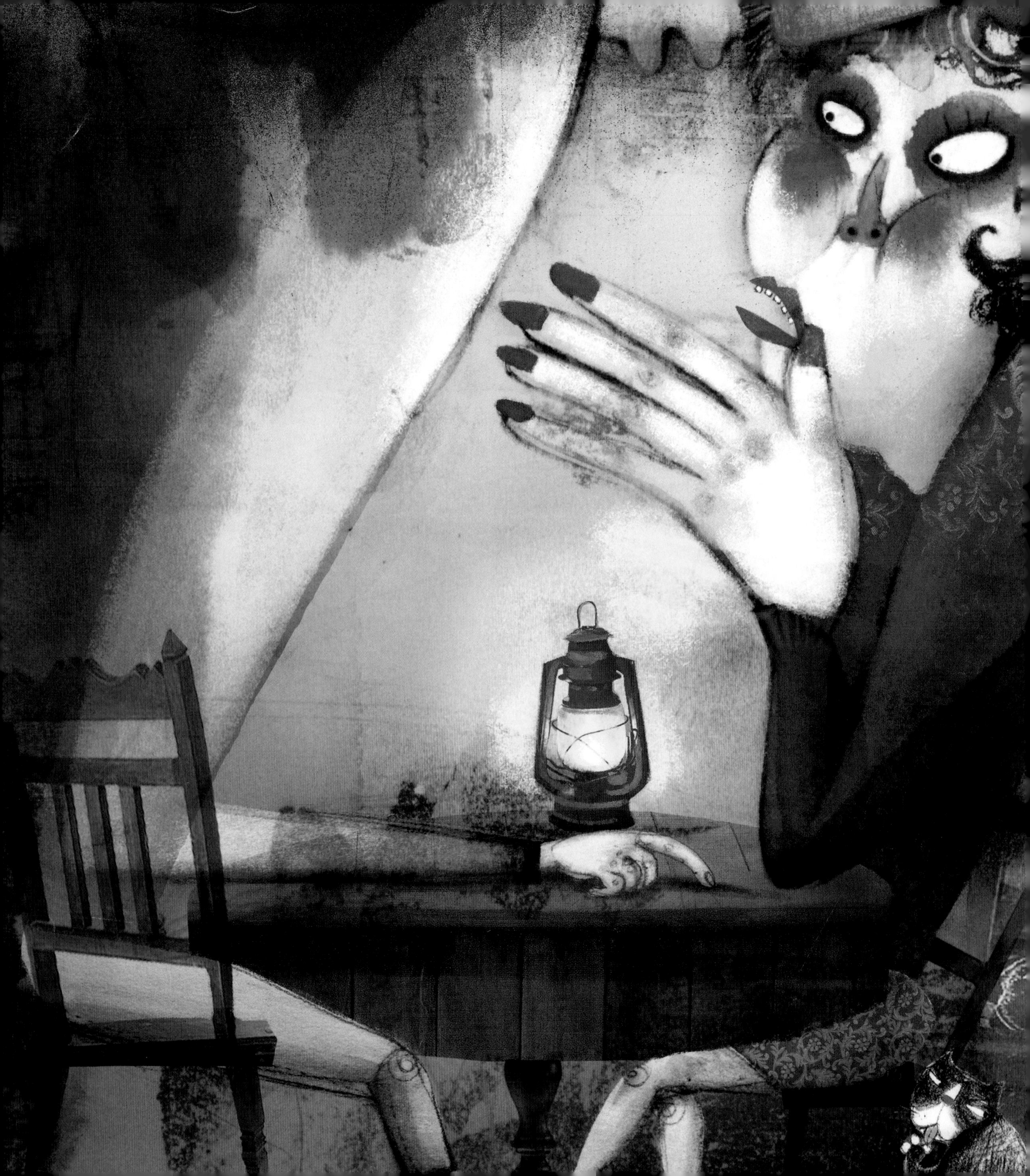

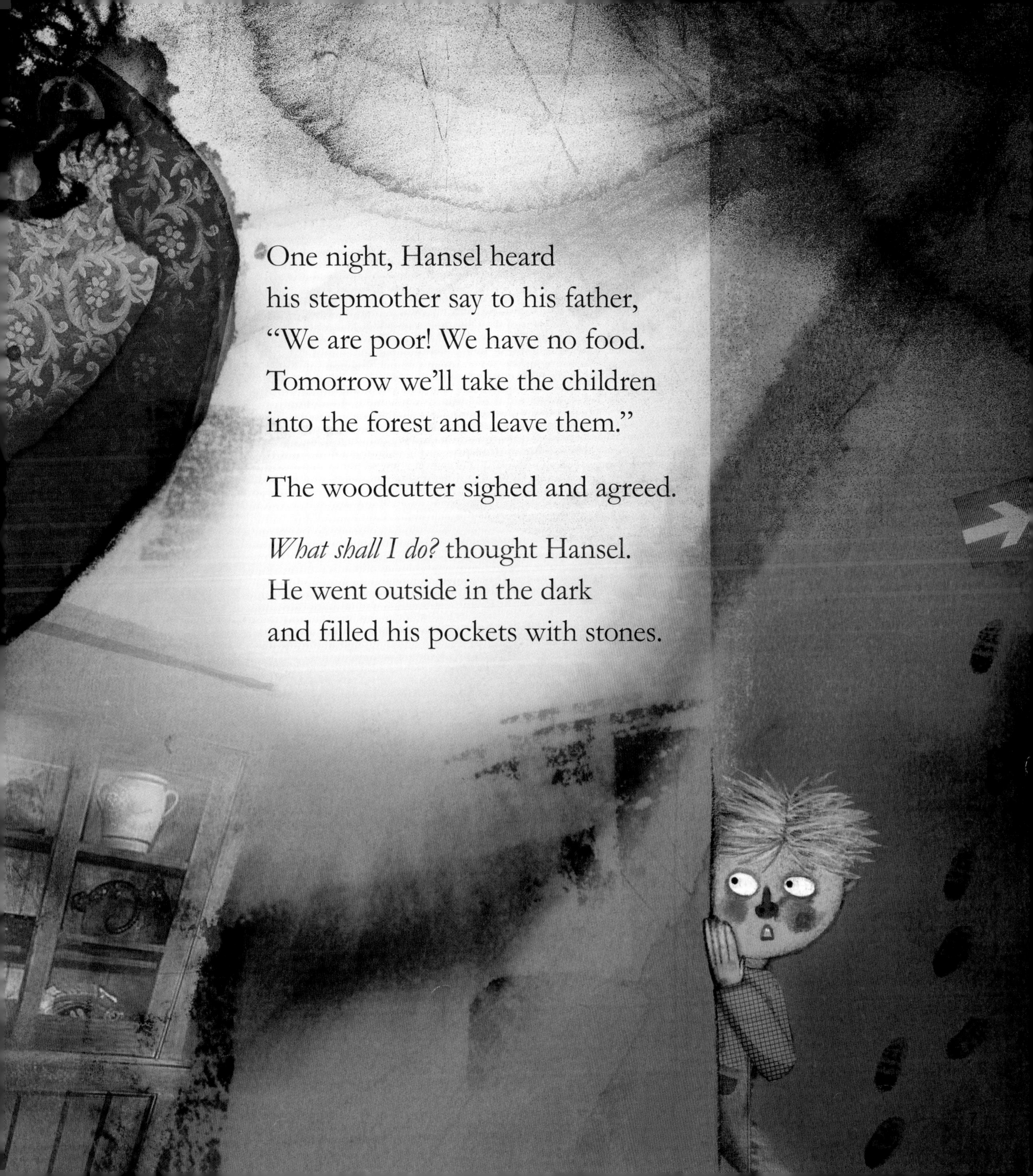

One night, Hansel heard
his stepmother say to his father,
"We are poor! We have no food.
Tomorrow we'll take the children
into the forest and leave them."

The woodcutter sighed and agreed.

*What shall I do?* thought Hansel.
He went outside in the dark
and filled his pockets with stones.

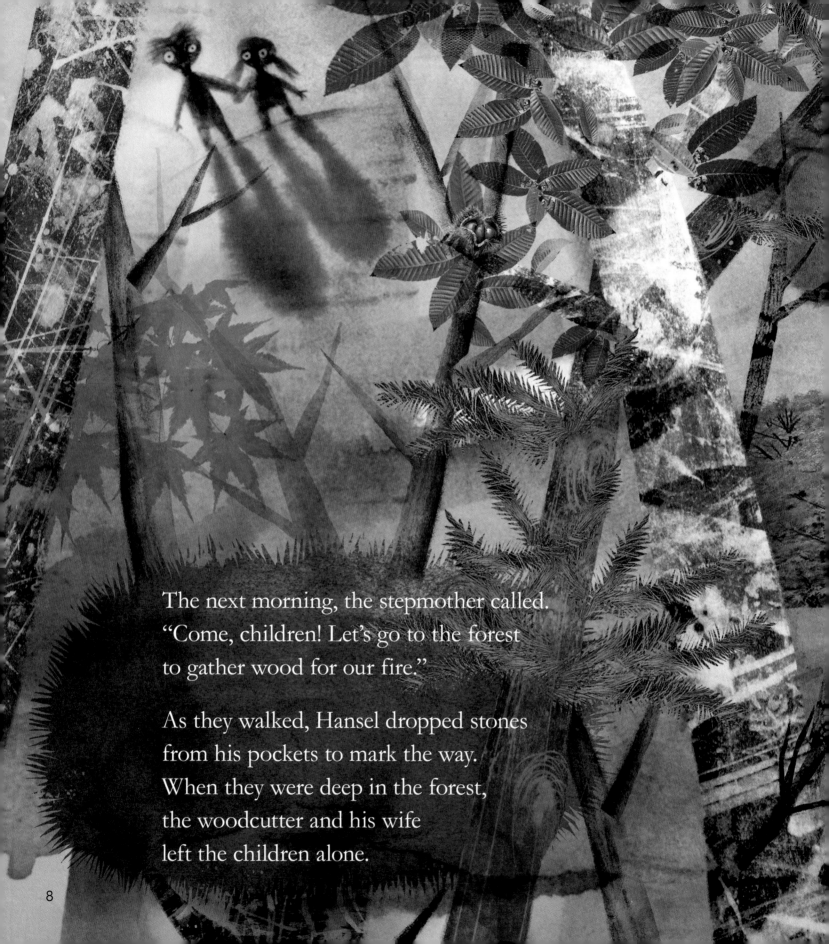

The next morning, the stepmother called.
"Come, children! Let's go to the forest
to gather wood for our fire."

As they walked, Hansel dropped stones
from his pockets to mark the way.
When they were deep in the forest,
the woodcutter and his wife
left the children alone.

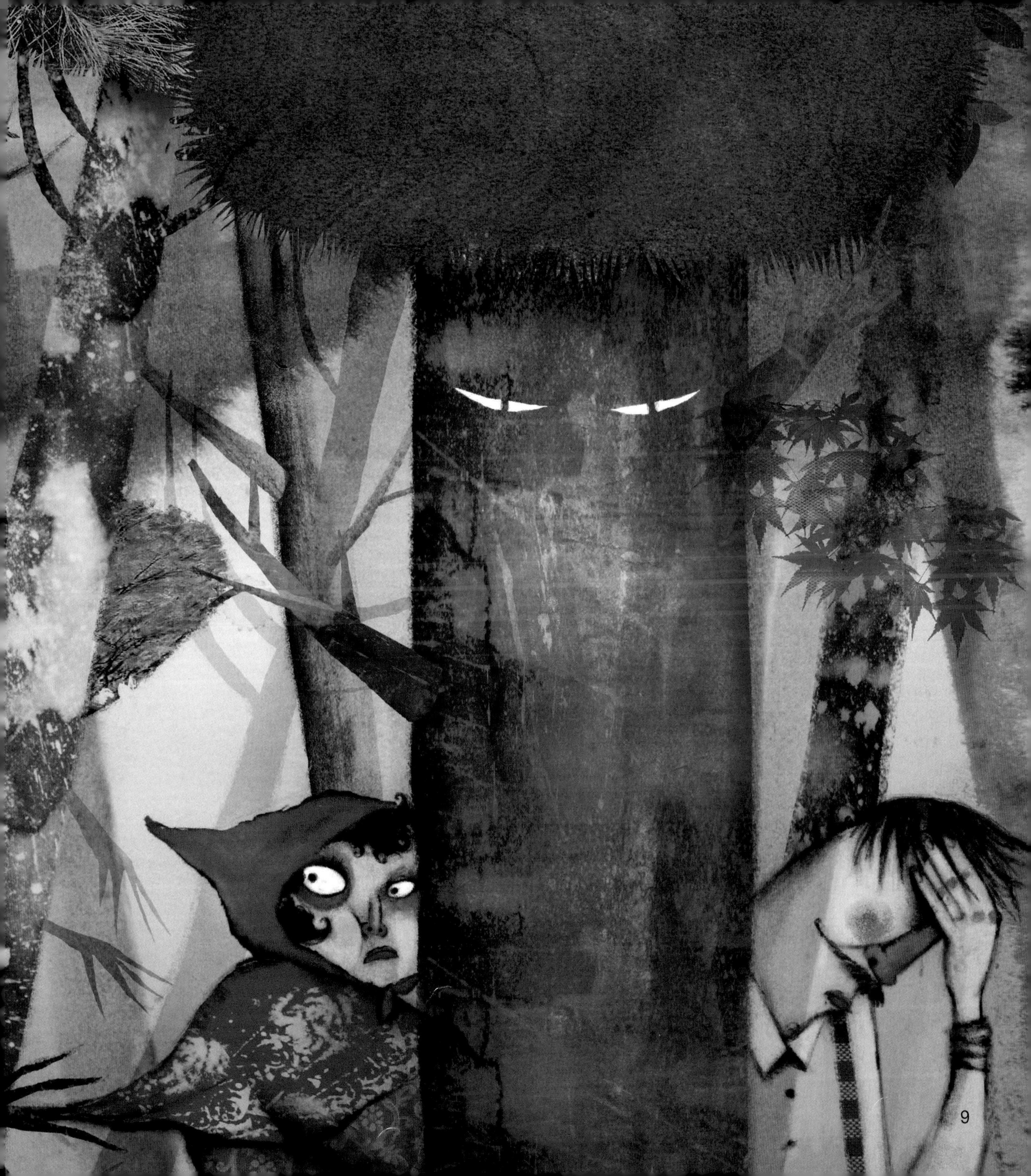

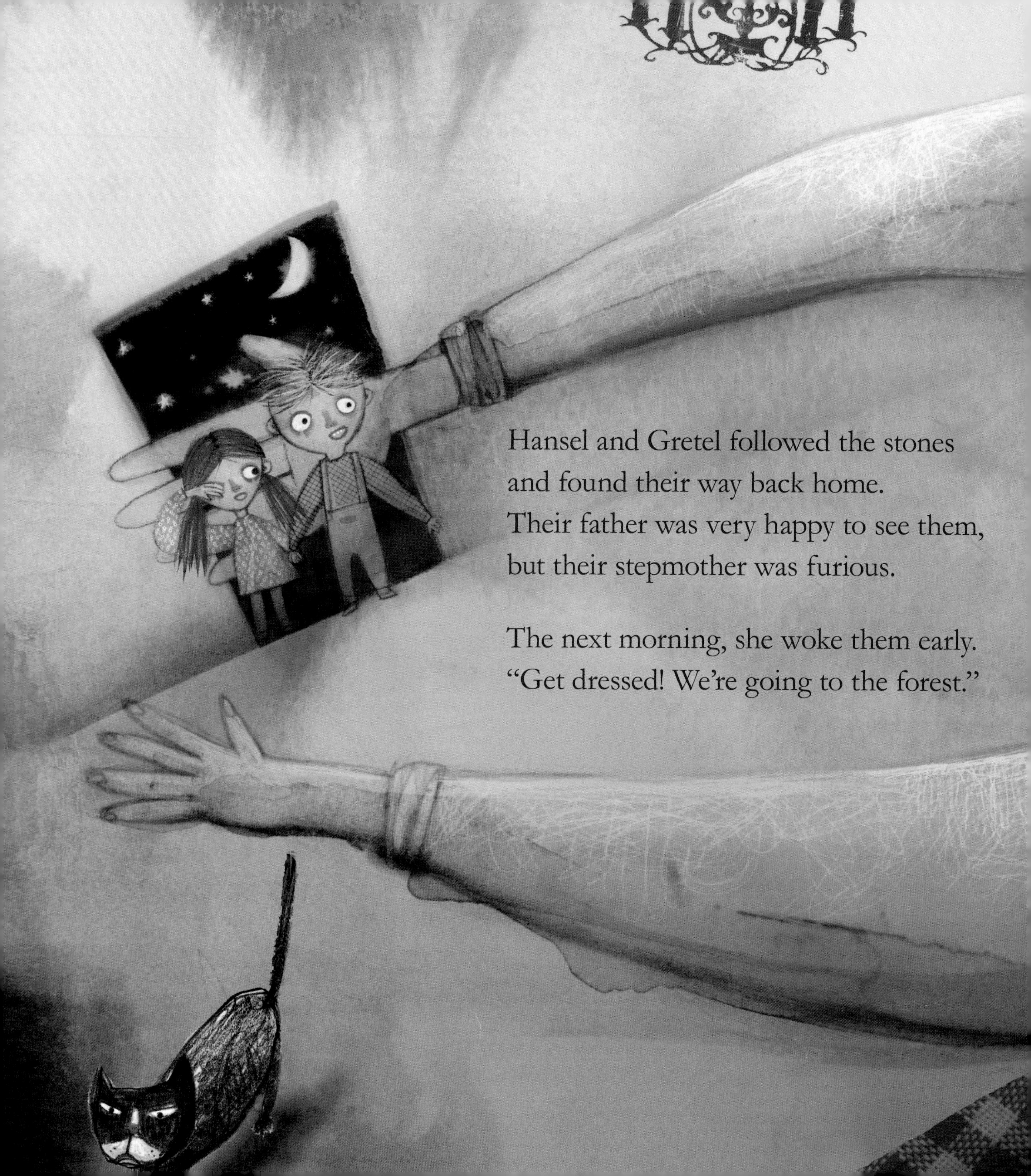

Hansel and Gretel followed the stones
and found their way back home.
Their father was very happy to see them,
but their stepmother was furious.

The next morning, she woke them early.
"Get dressed! We're going to the forest."

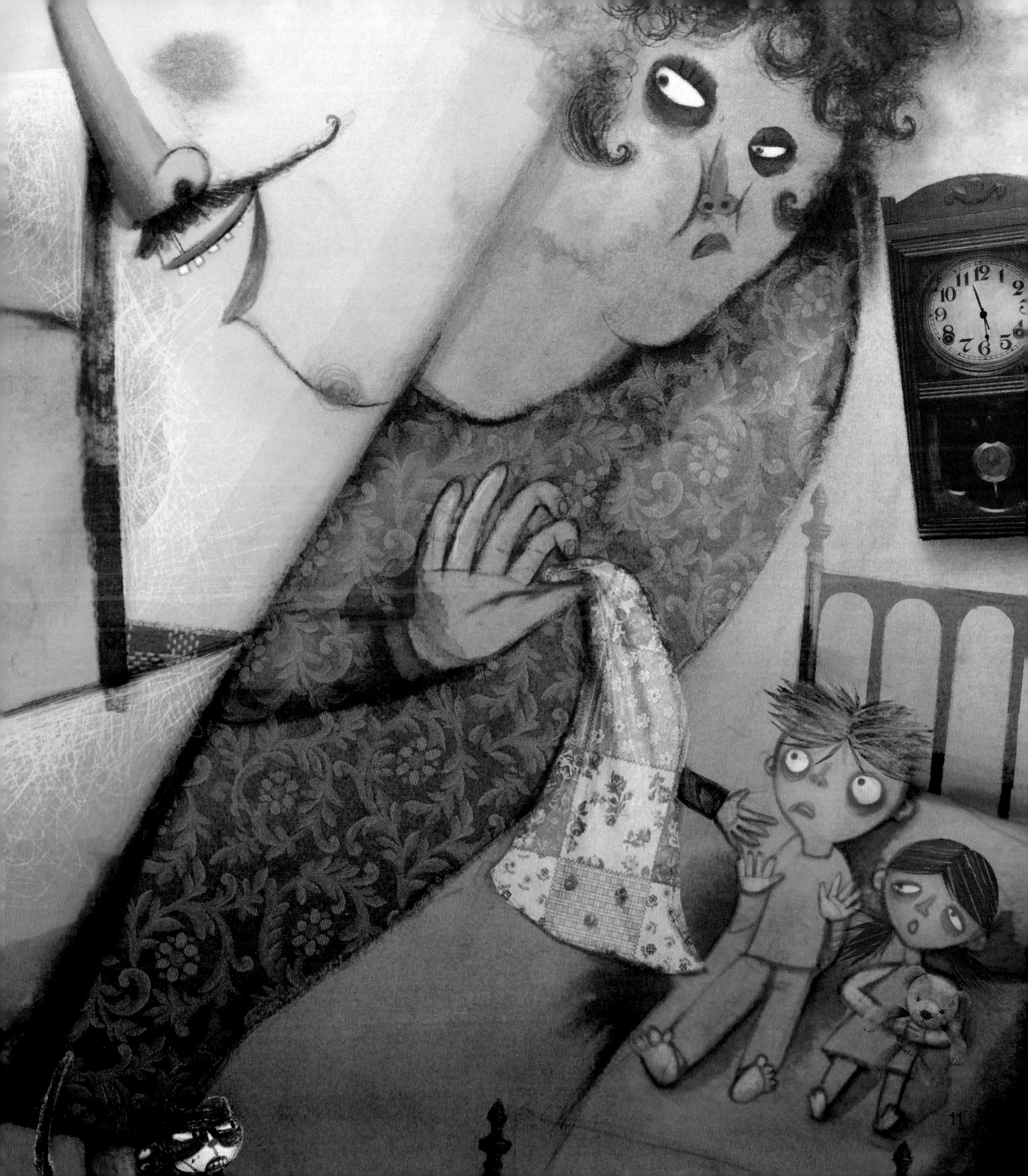

12
1
2
3
4
5
6
7
8
9
10
11

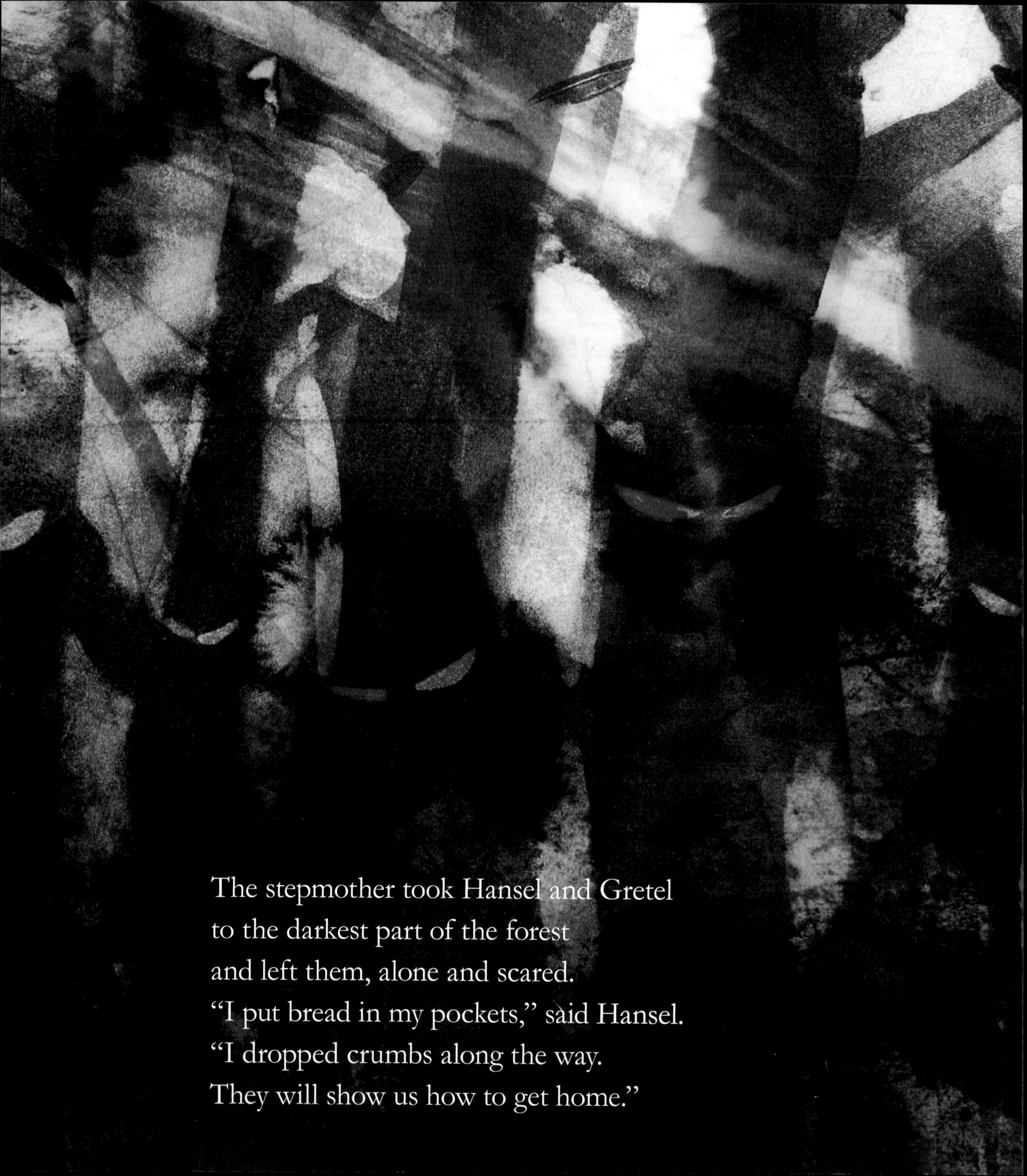

The stepmother took Hansel and Gretel
to the darkest part of the forest
and left them, alone and scared.
"I put bread in my pockets," said Hansel.
"I dropped crumbs along the way.
They will show us how to get home."

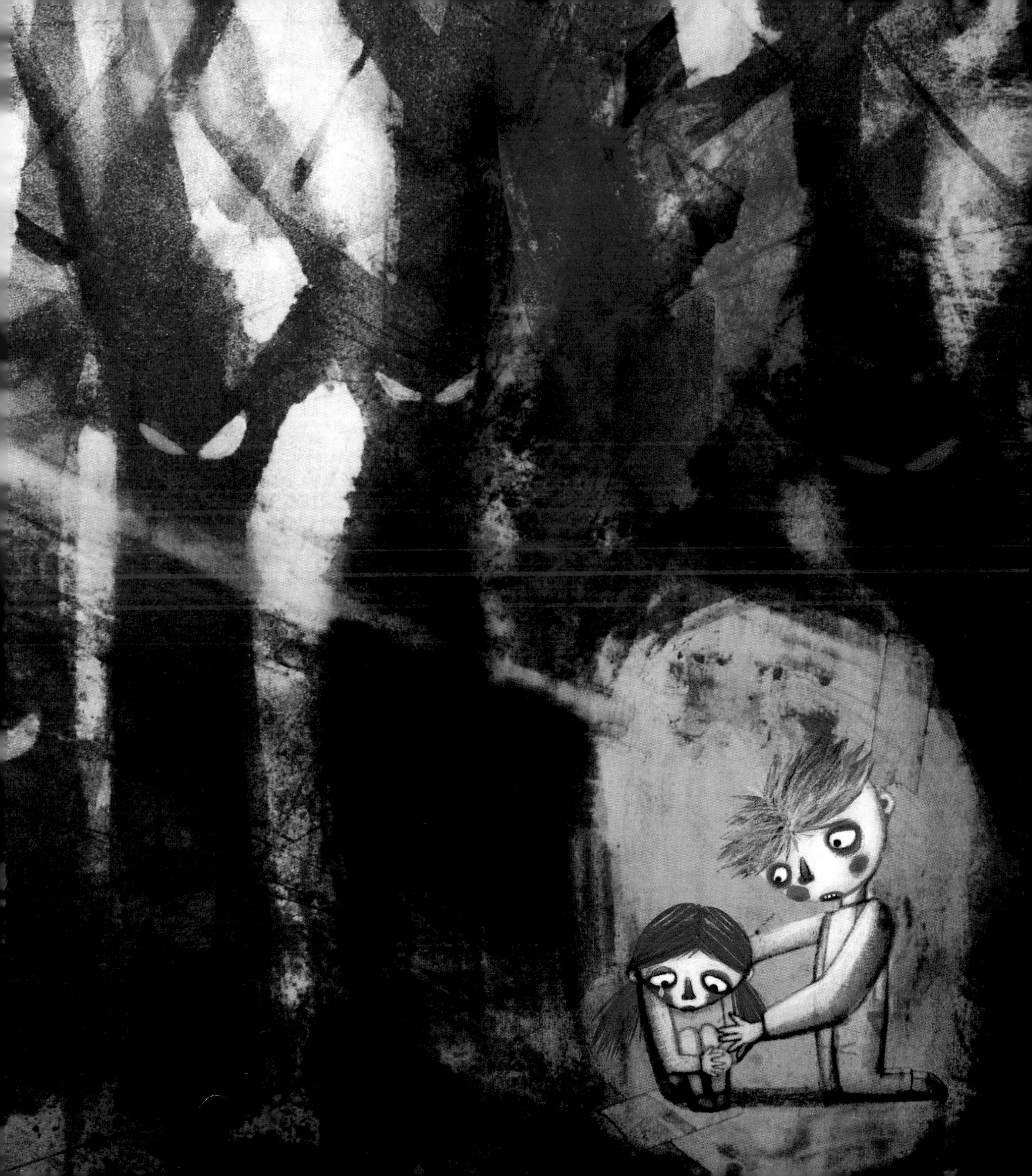

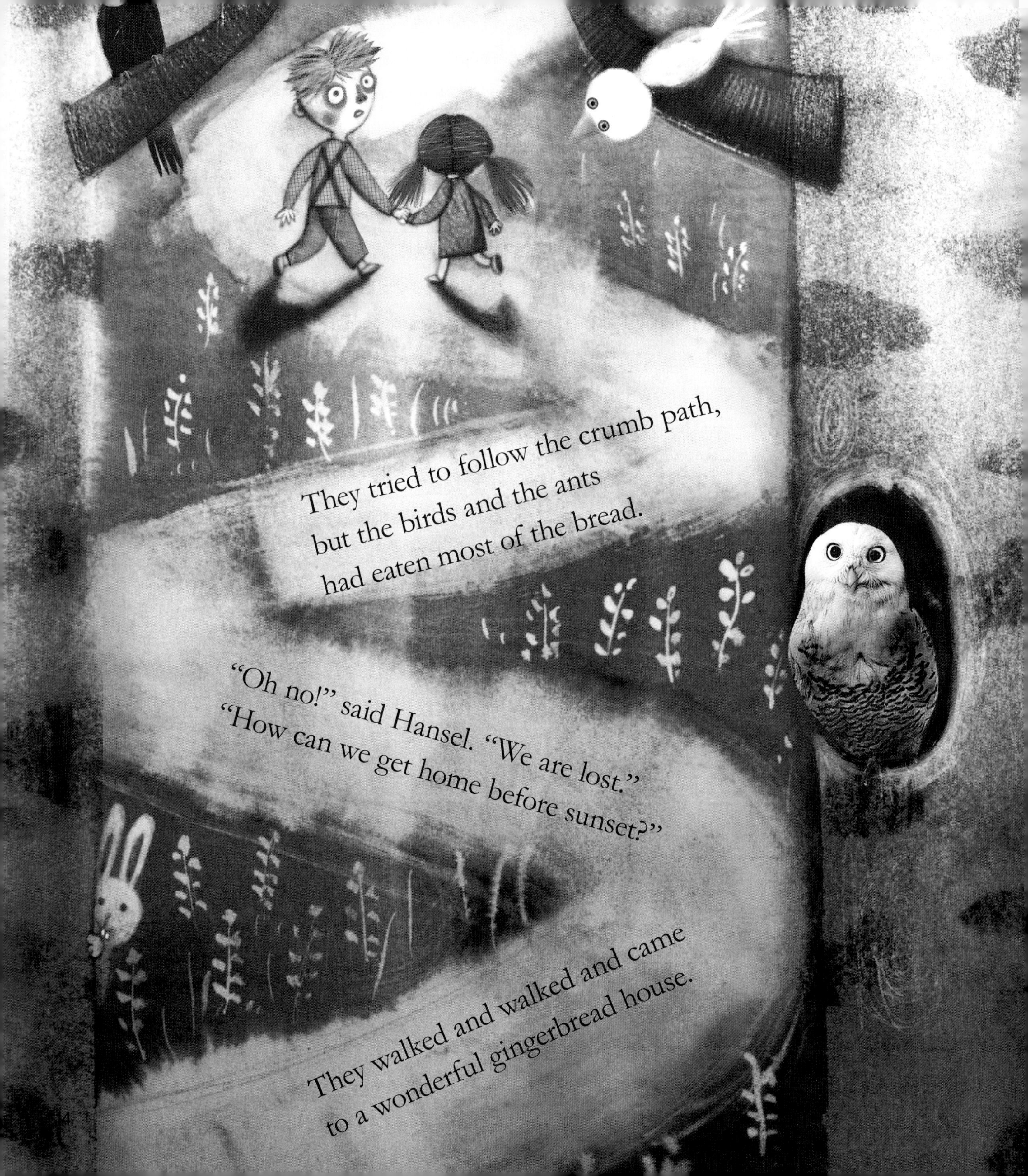

They tried to follow the crumb path,
but the birds and the ants
had eaten most of the bread.

"Oh no!" said Hansel. "We are lost."
"How can we get home before sunset?"

They walked and walked and came
to a wonderful gingerbread house.

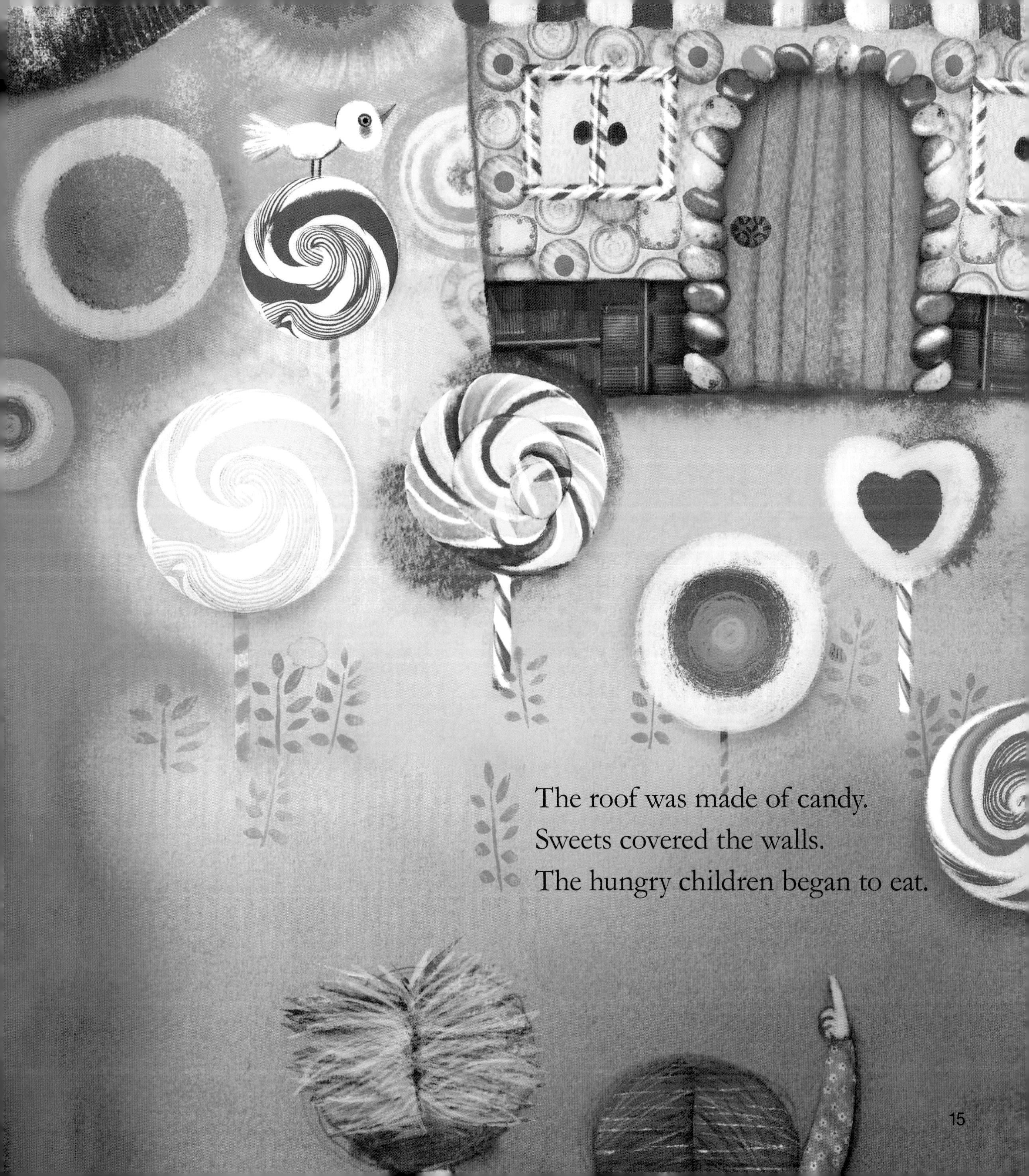

The roof was made of candy.
Sweets covered the walls.
The hungry children began to eat.

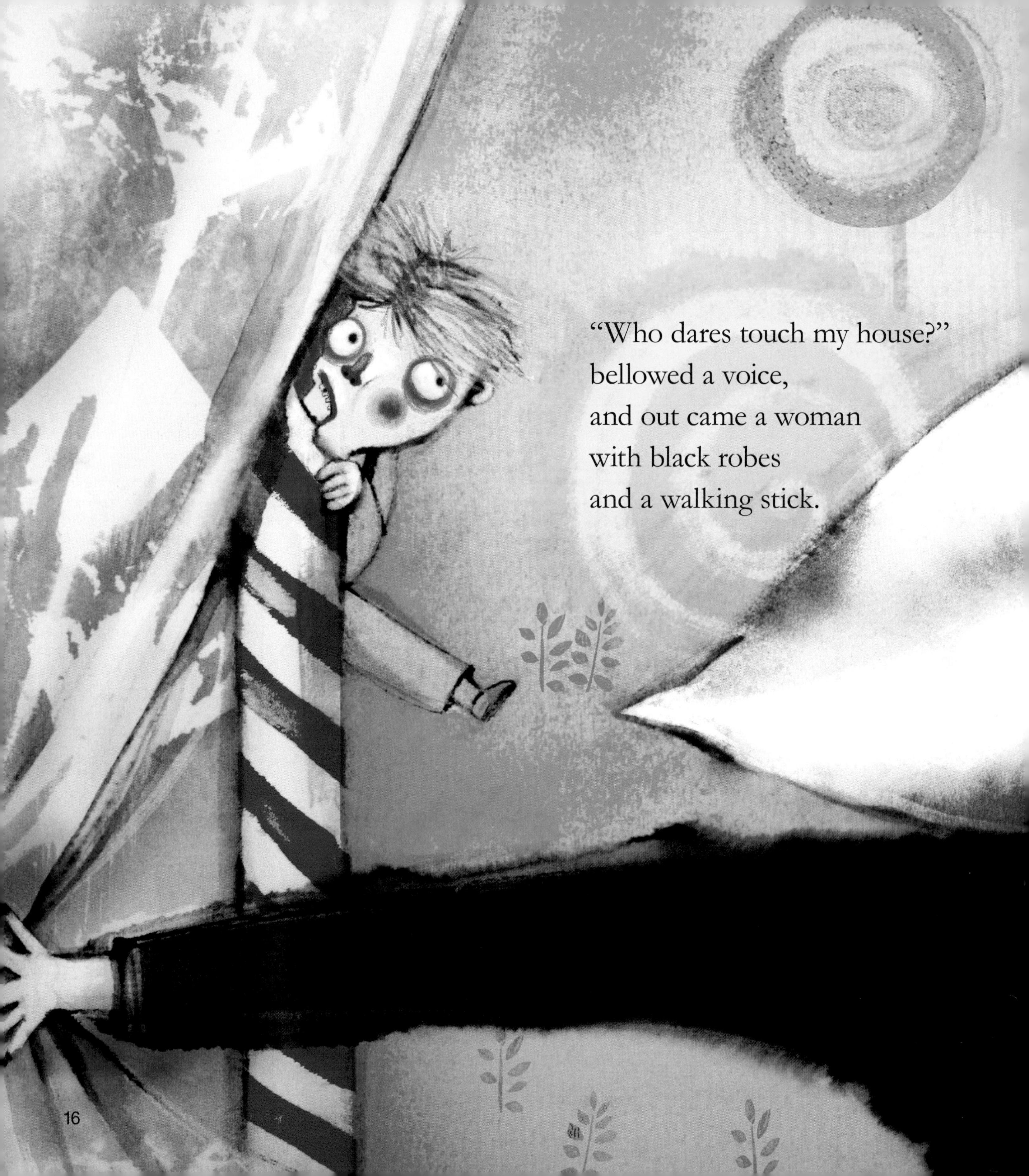

"Who dares touch my house?"
bellowed a voice,
and out came a woman
with black robes
and a walking stick.

“We lost our way in the woods,”
said Gretel. “We were hungry.”

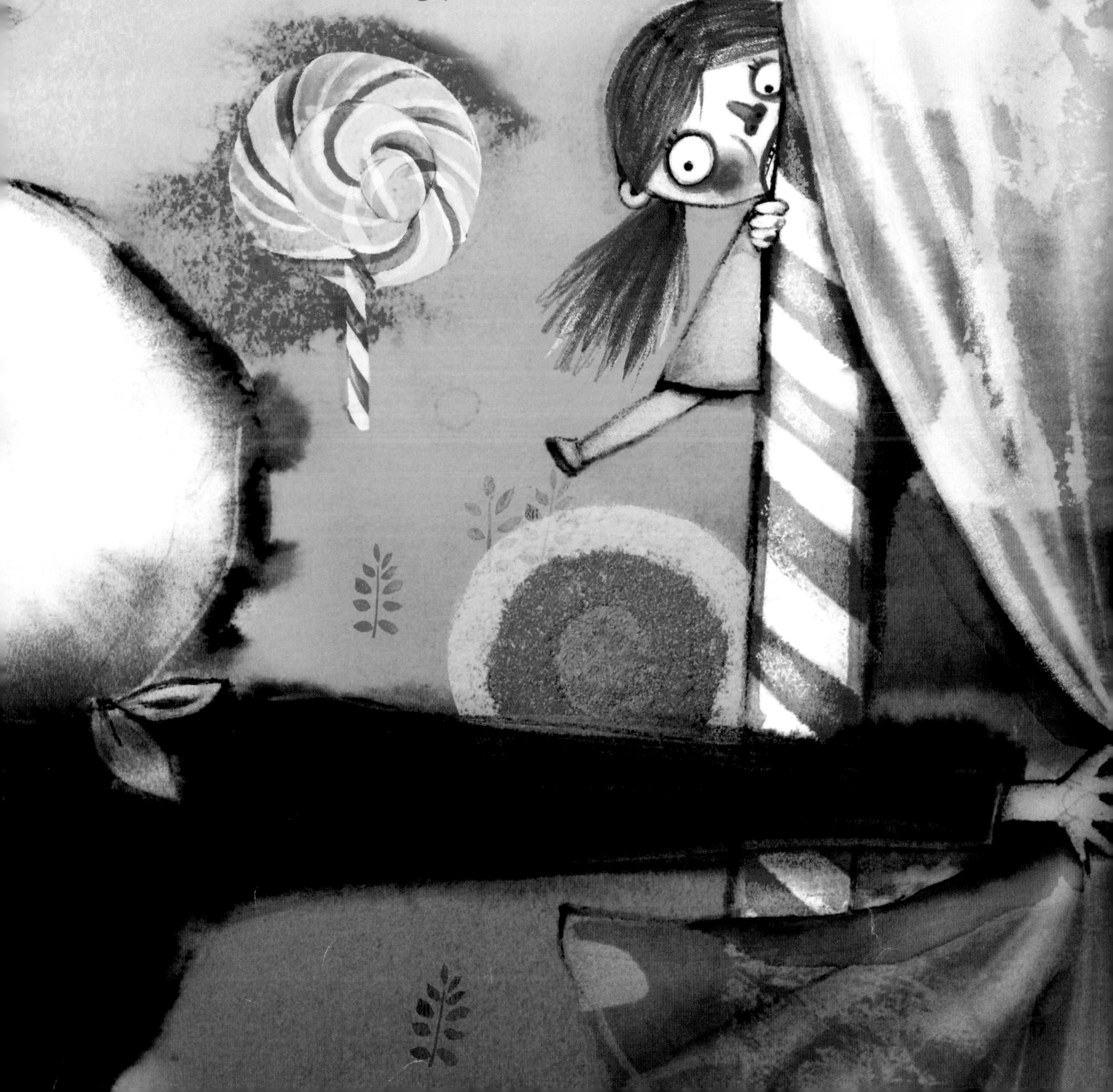

The woman smiled. “Well, well!
You don’t say! Come in, children.
Make yourself at home.”

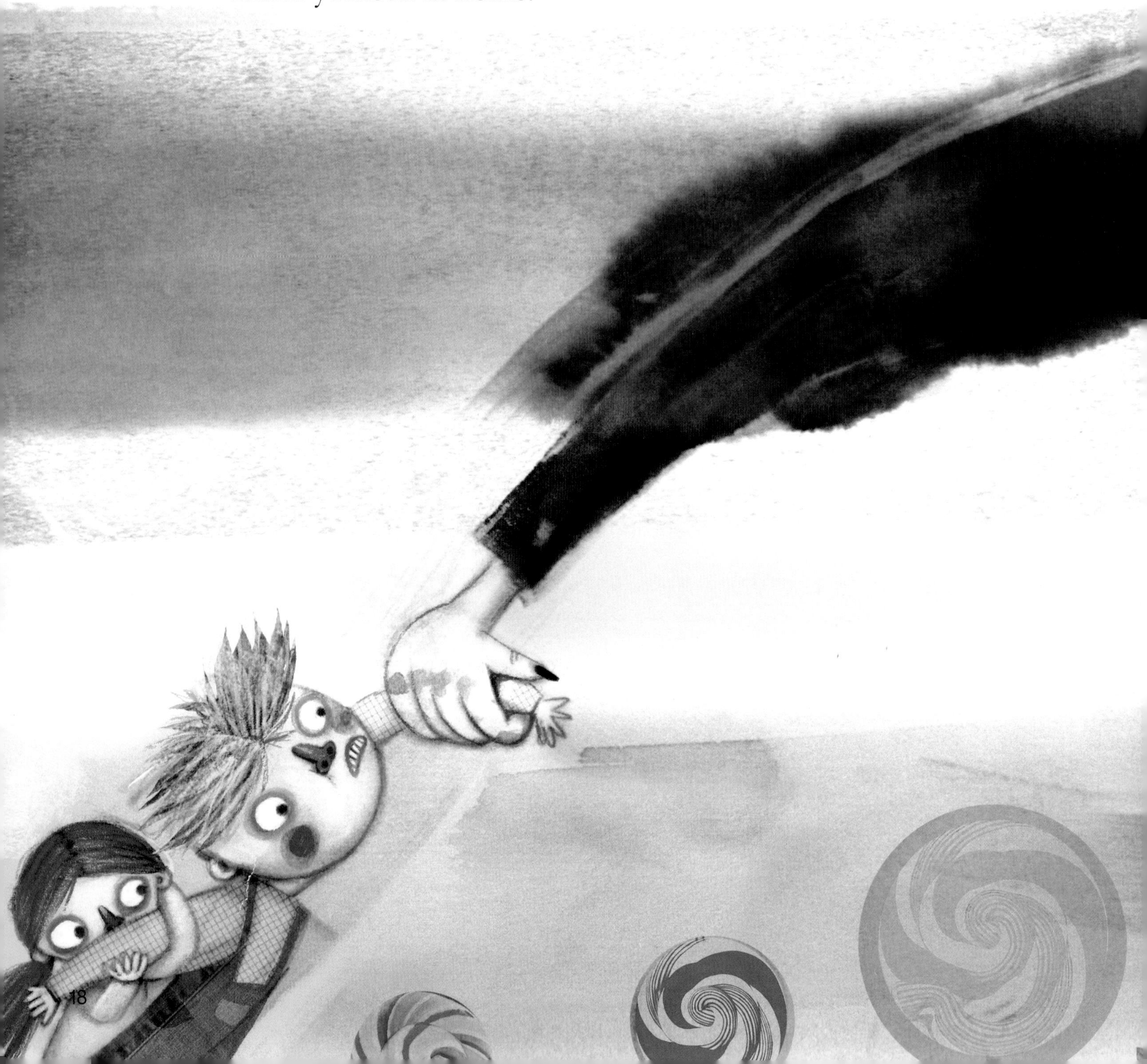

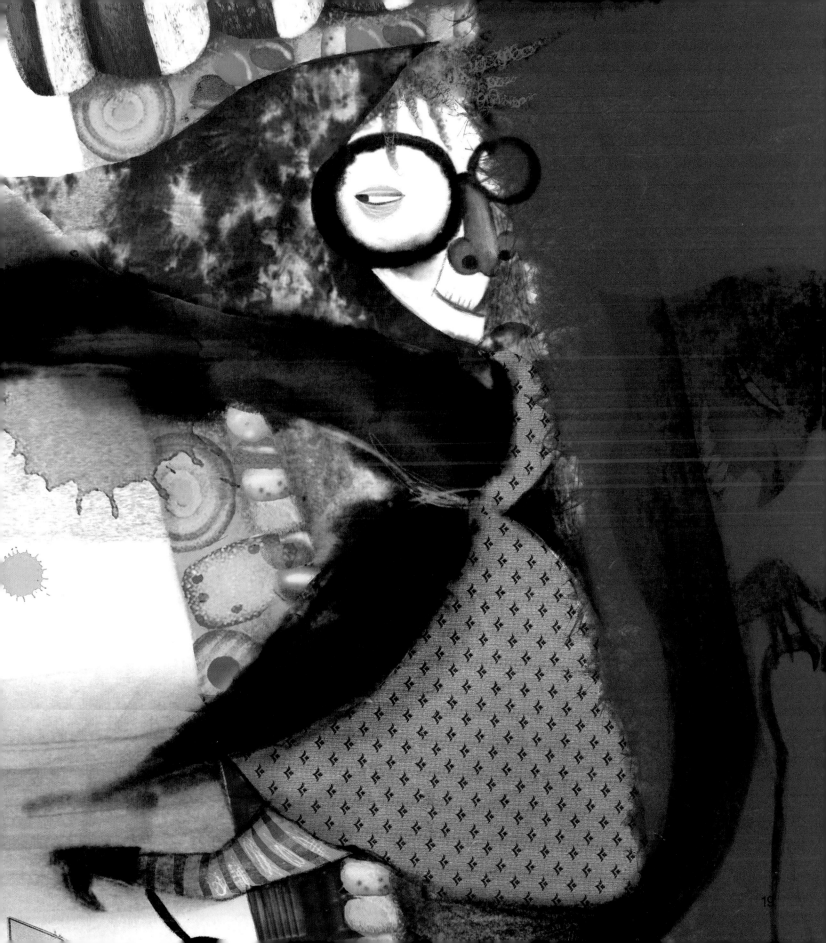

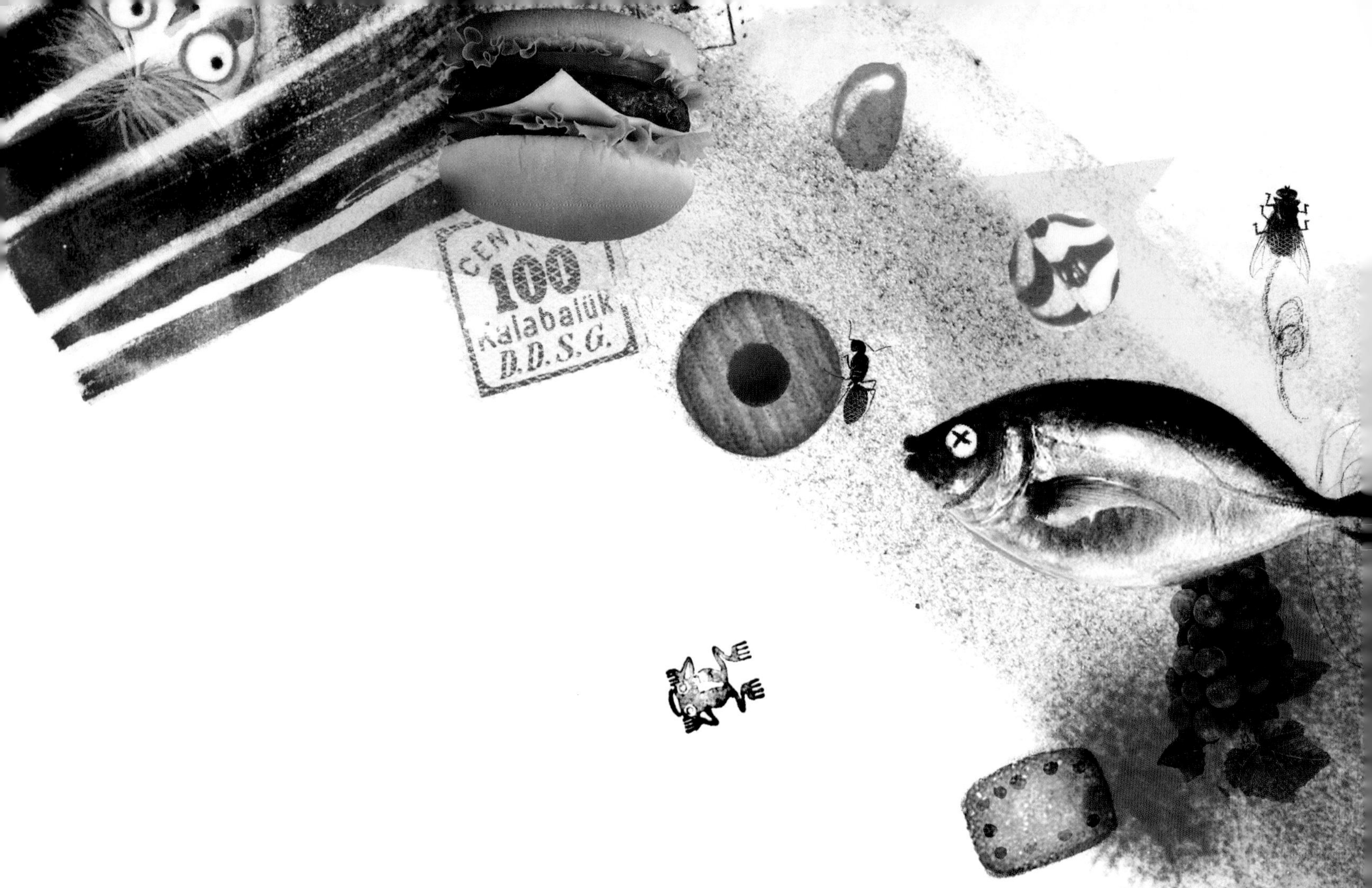
100
Kalabalük
D.D.S.G.

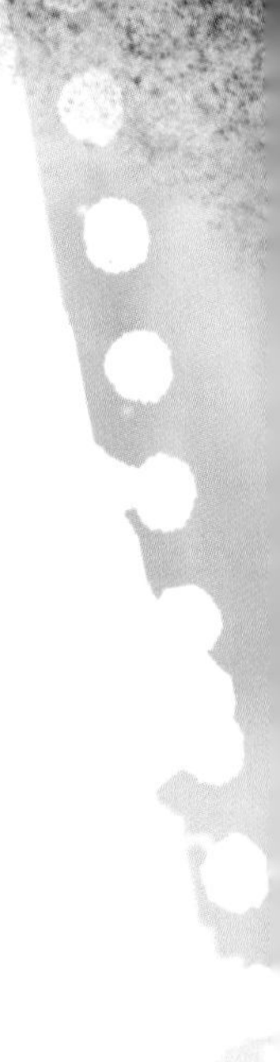

The next day, the old woman
locked Hansel in a cage.
She pushed food at him
through the bars.

Gretel was forced
to be the woman's servant.
She worked hard all day.

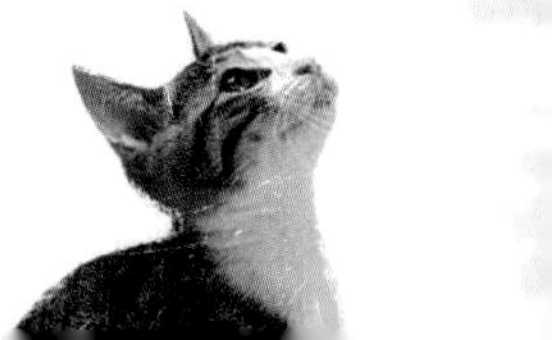

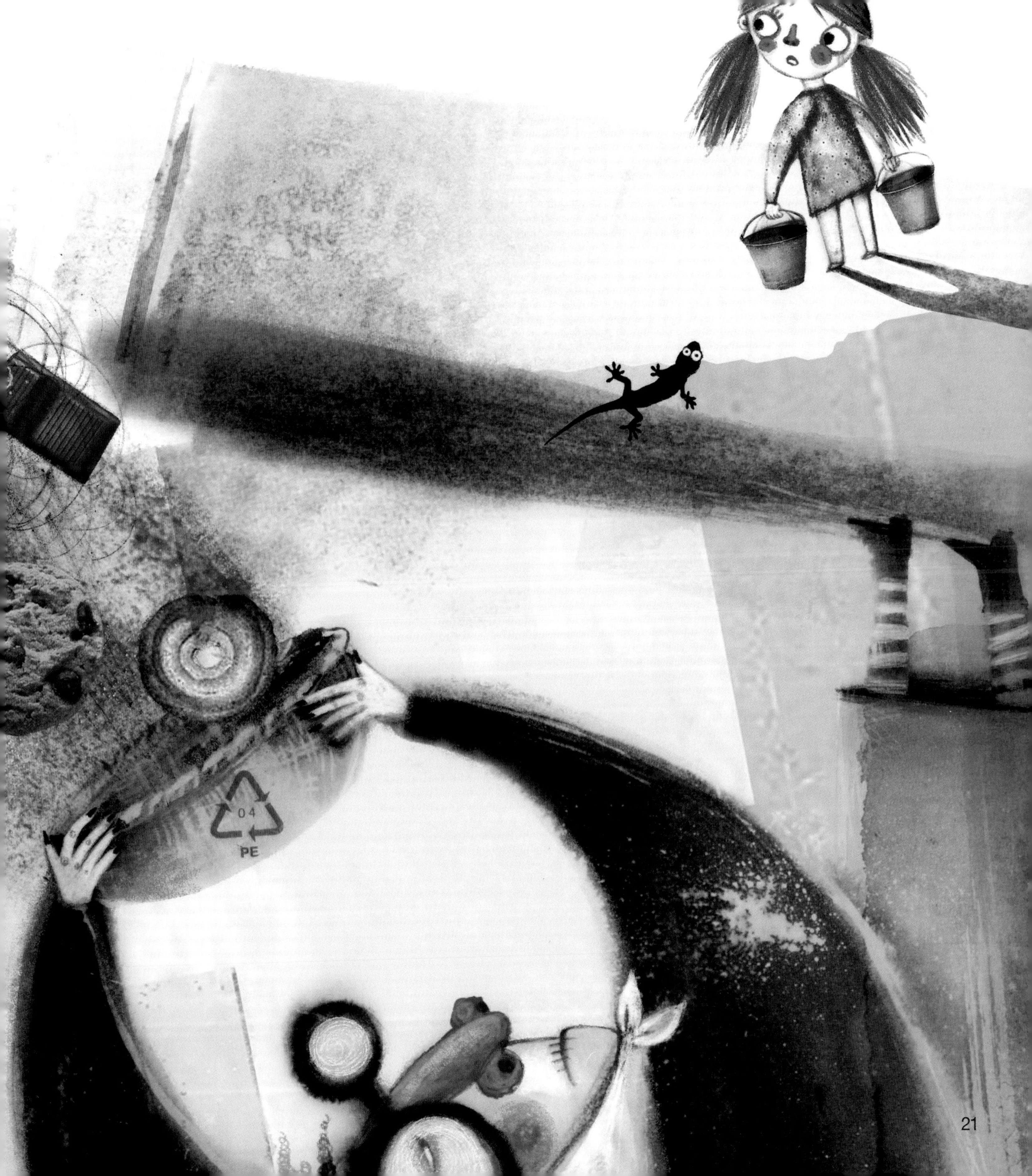
04
PE

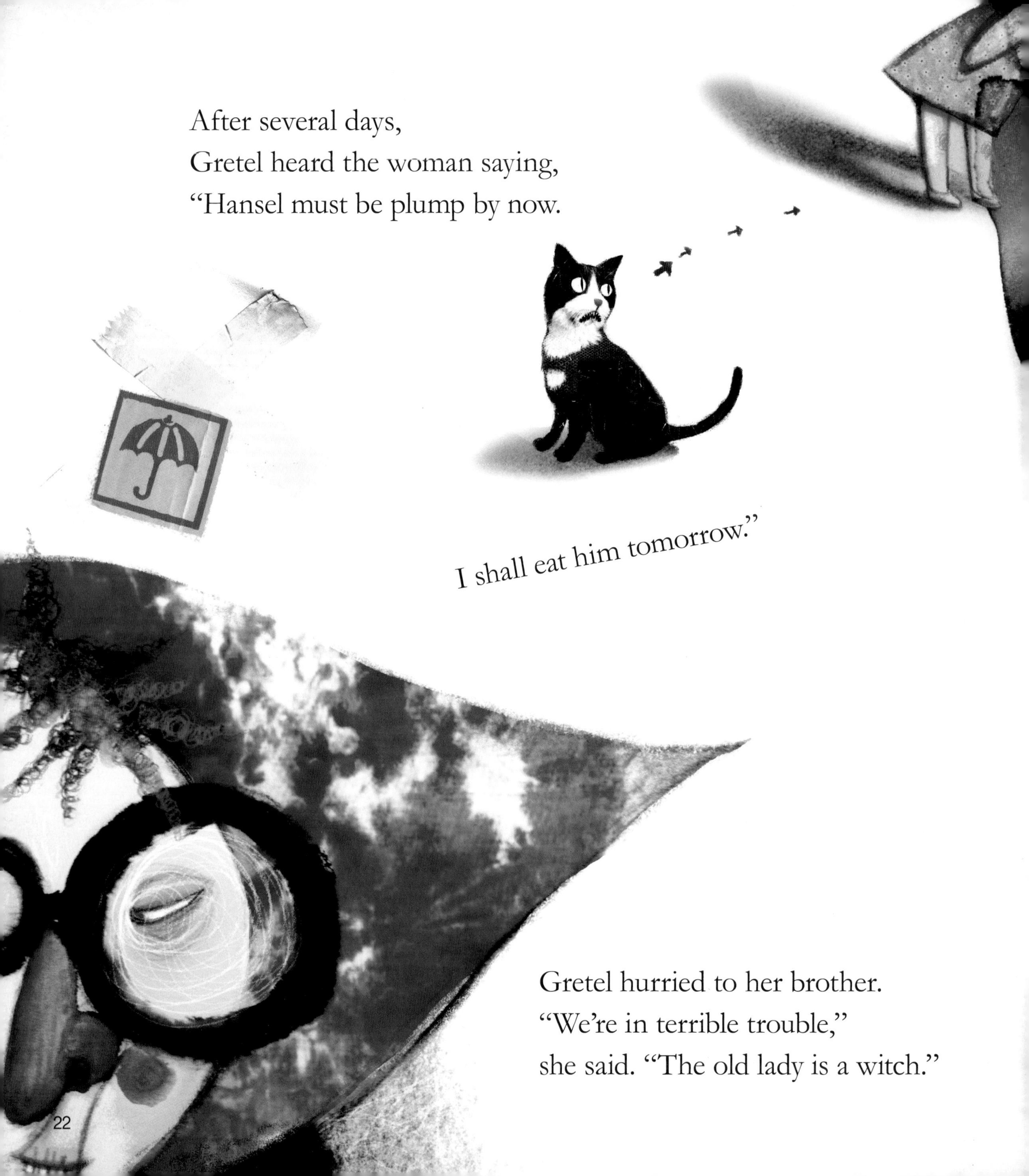

After several days,
Gretel heard the woman saying,
"Hansel must be plump by now.

I shall eat him tomorrow."

Gretel hurried to her brother.
"We're in terrible trouble,"
she said. "The old lady is a witch."

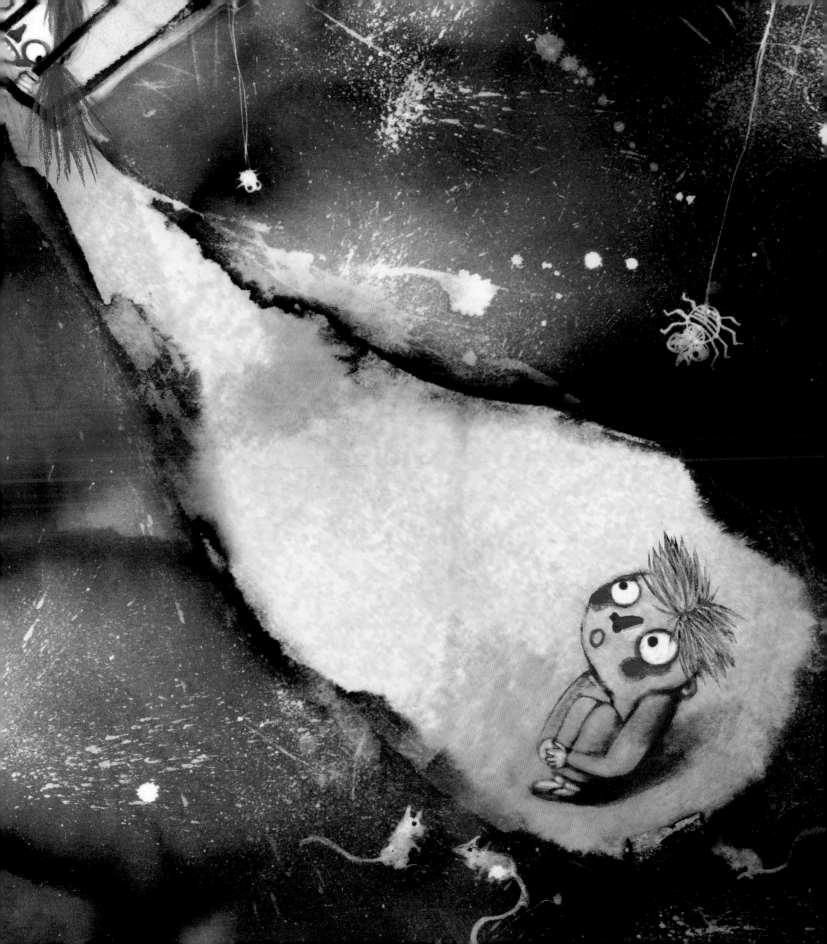

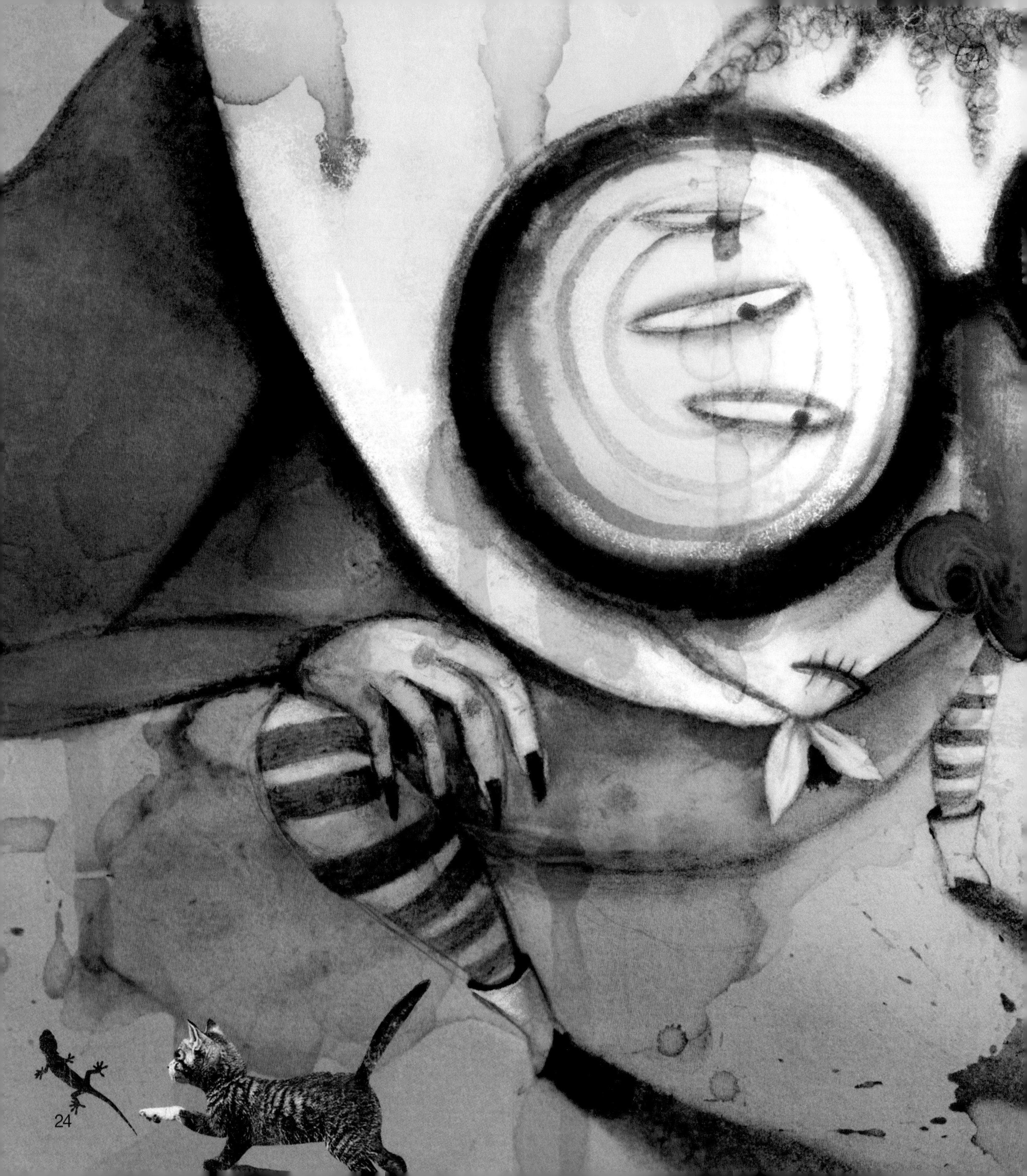

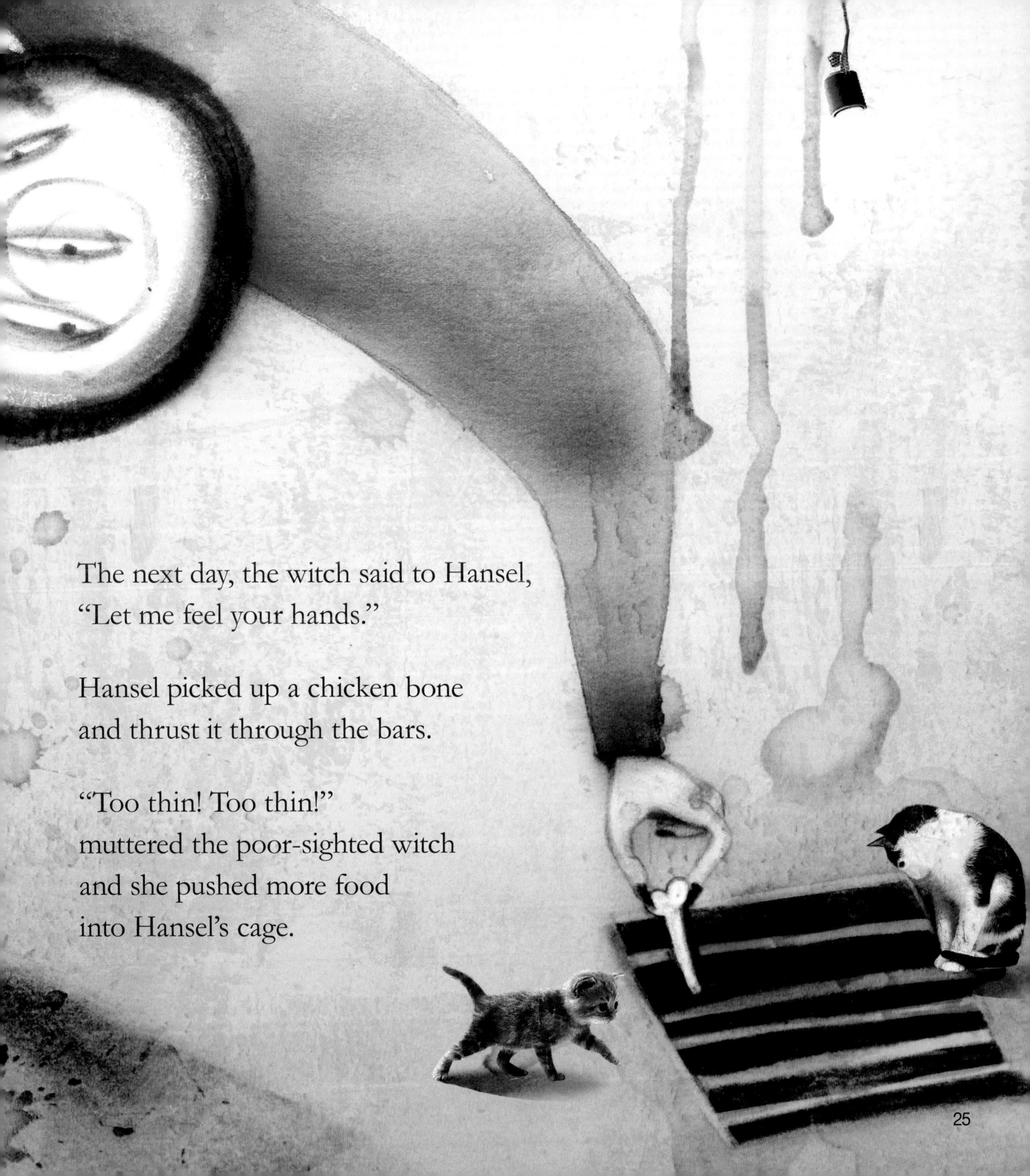

The next day, the witch said to Hansel,
"Let me feel your hands."

Hansel picked up a chicken bone
and thrust it through the bars.

"Too thin! Too thin!"
muttered the poor-sighted witch
and she pushed more food
into Hansel's cage.

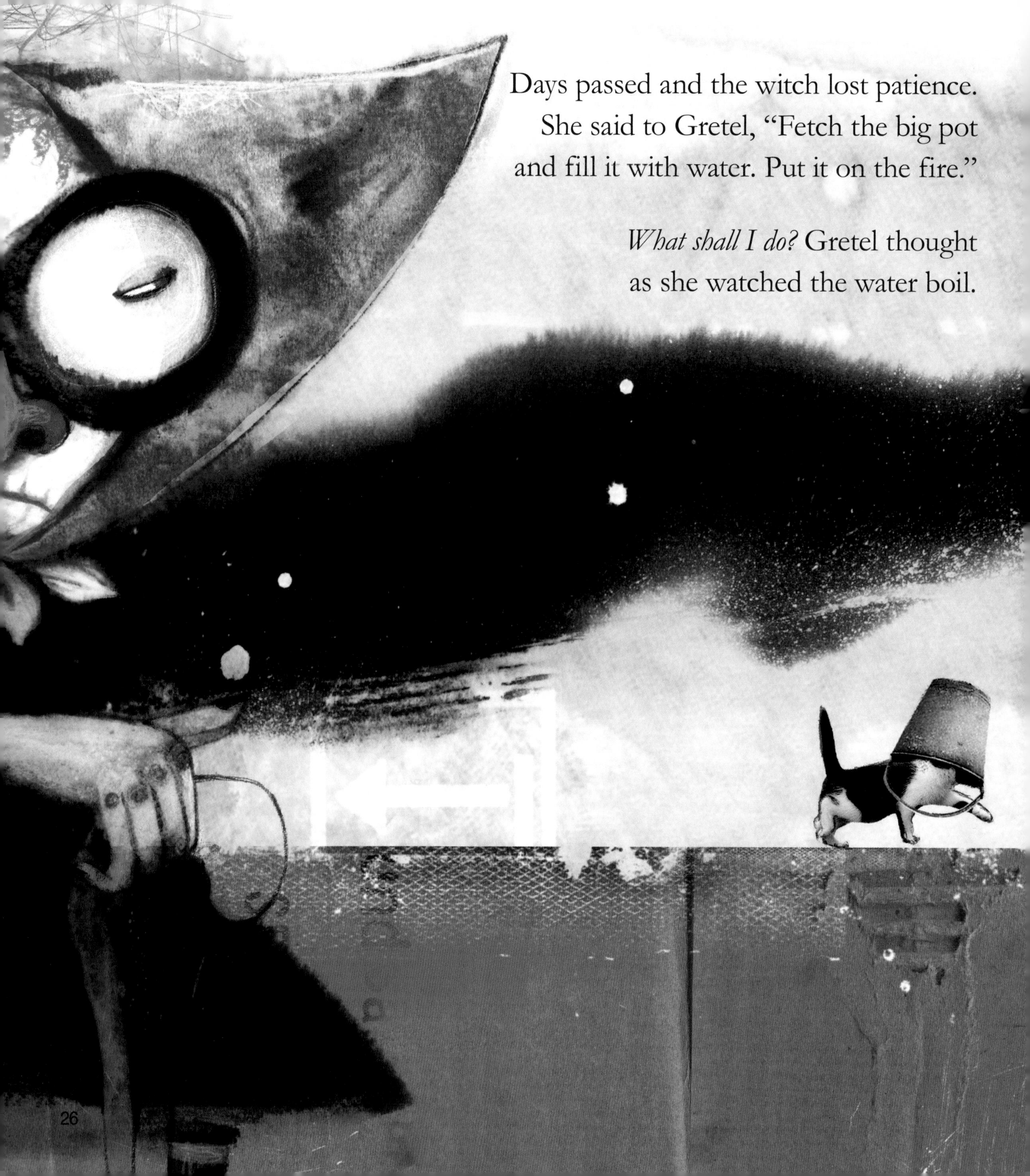

Days passed and the witch lost patience. She said to Gretel, “Fetch the big pot and fill it with water. Put it on the fire.”

*What shall I do?* Gretel thought as she watched the water boil.

"Is it boiling yet?" screeched the witch.

"I don't know," Gretel said.
"Can you come and help me?"

"Stupid girl! Get out of the way!"
The witch ran to the boiling pot.

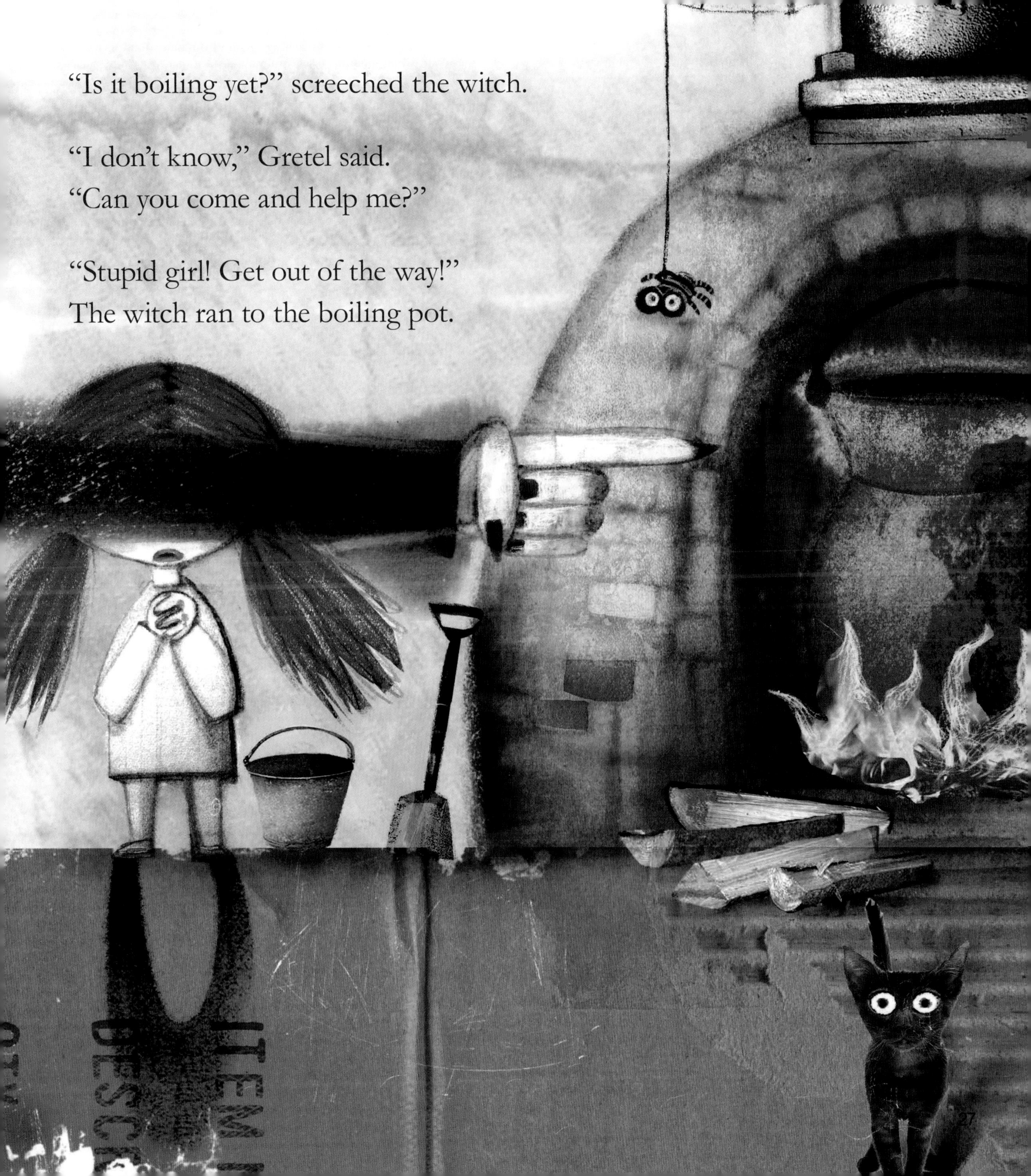

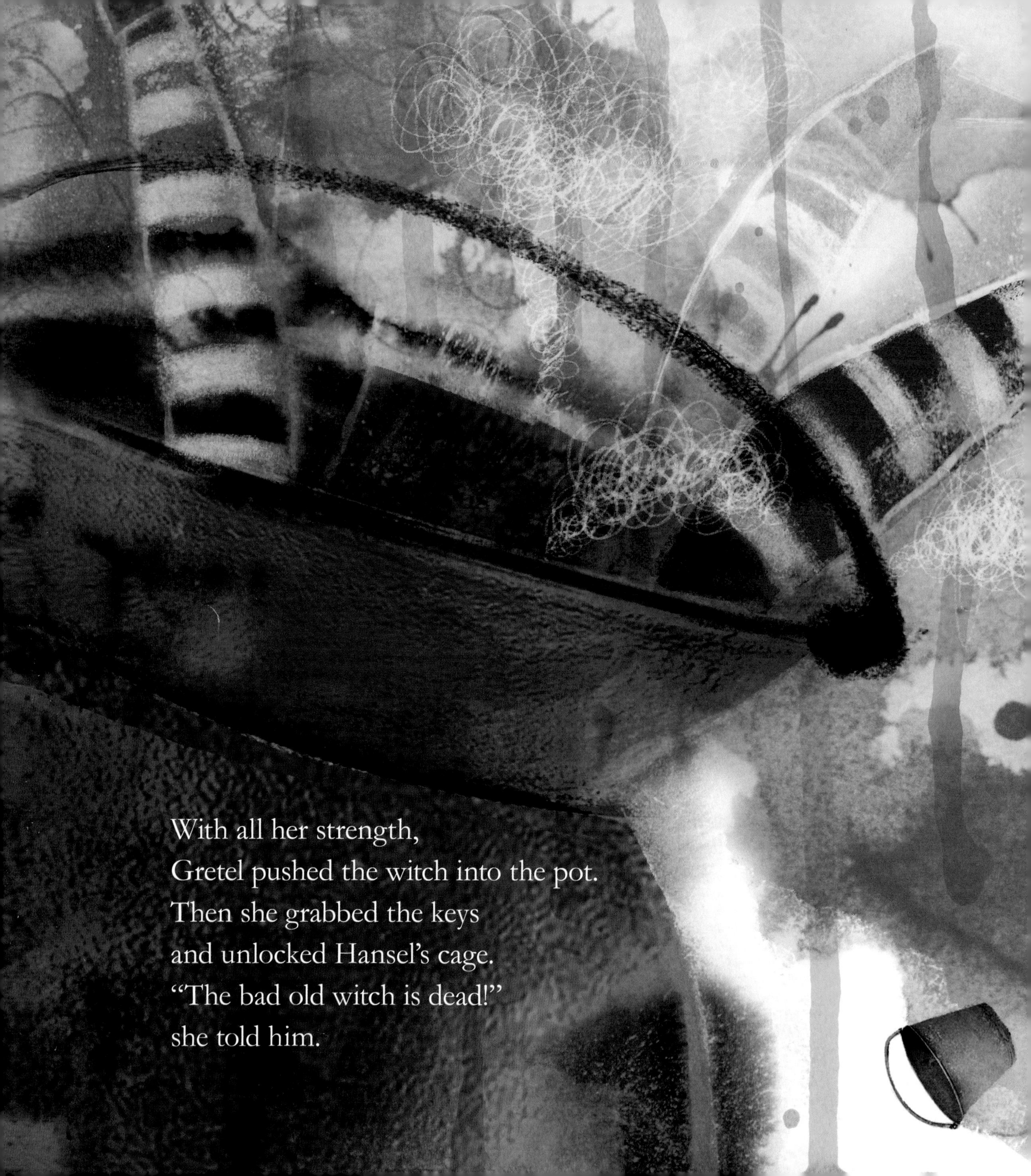

With all her strength,
Gretel pushed the witch into the pot.
Then she grabbed the keys
and unlocked Hansel's cage.
"The bad old witch is dead!"
she told him.

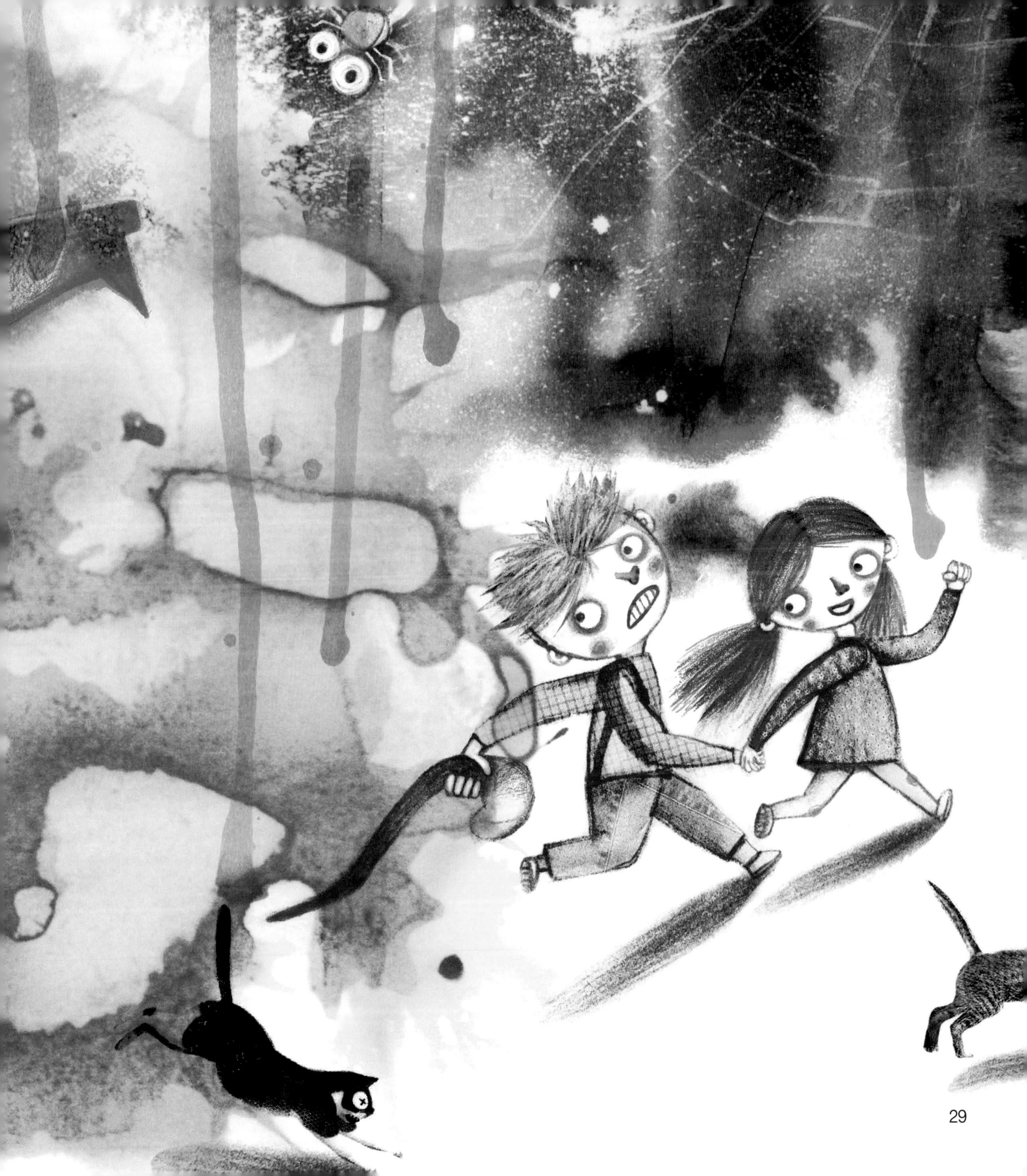

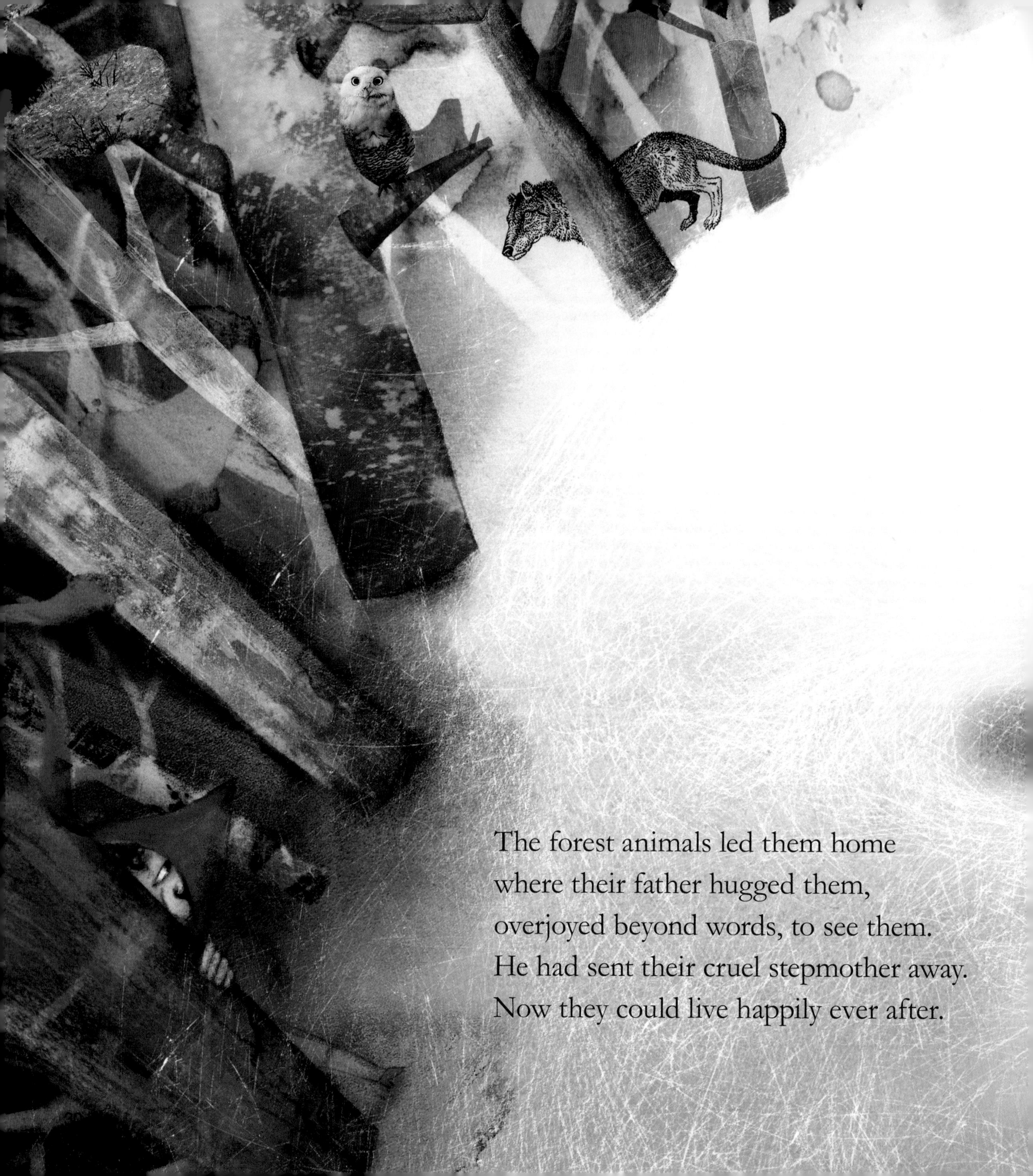

The forest animals led them home
where their father hugged them,
overjoyed beyond words, to see them.
He had sent their cruel stepmother away.
Now they could live happily ever after.

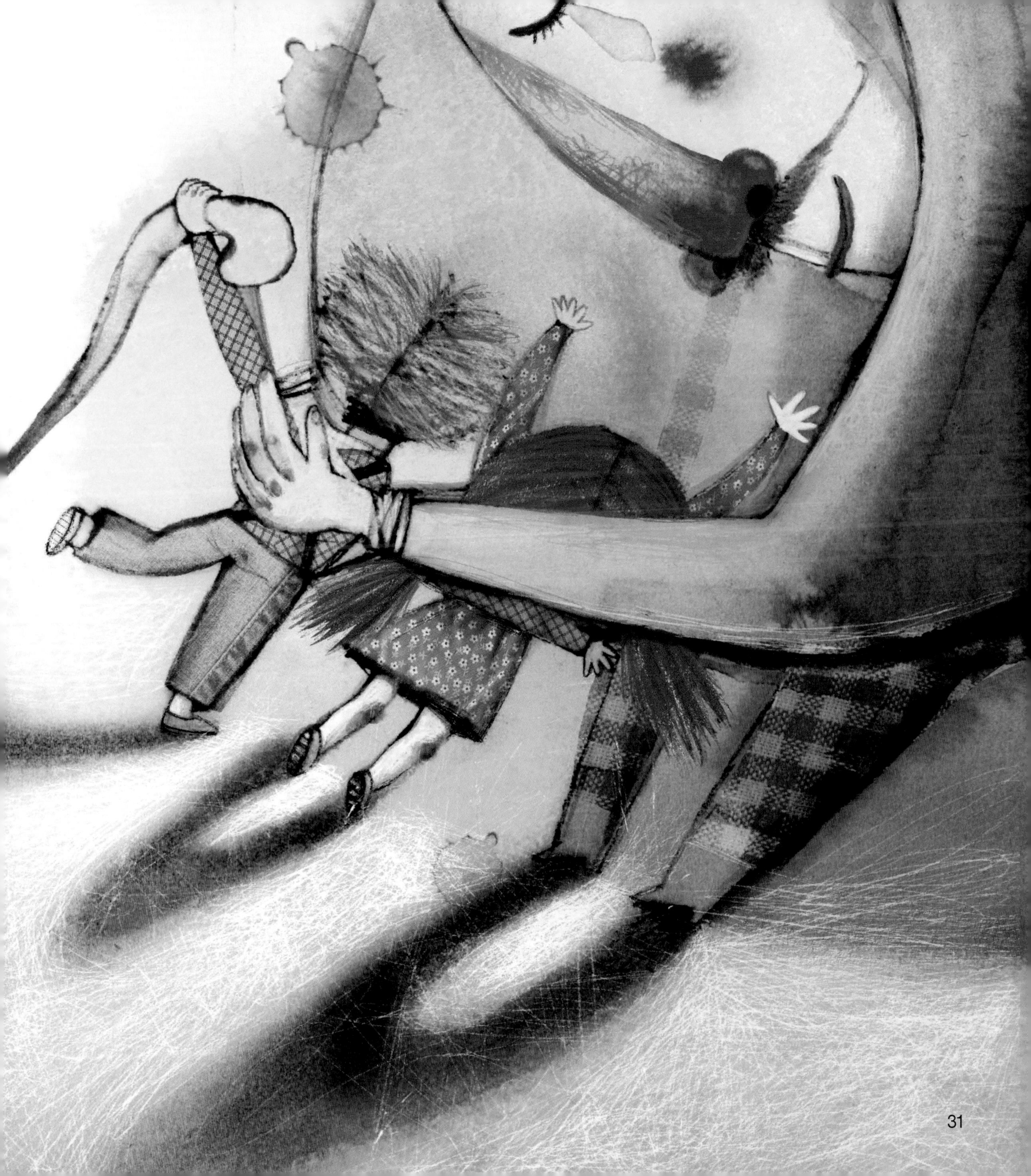

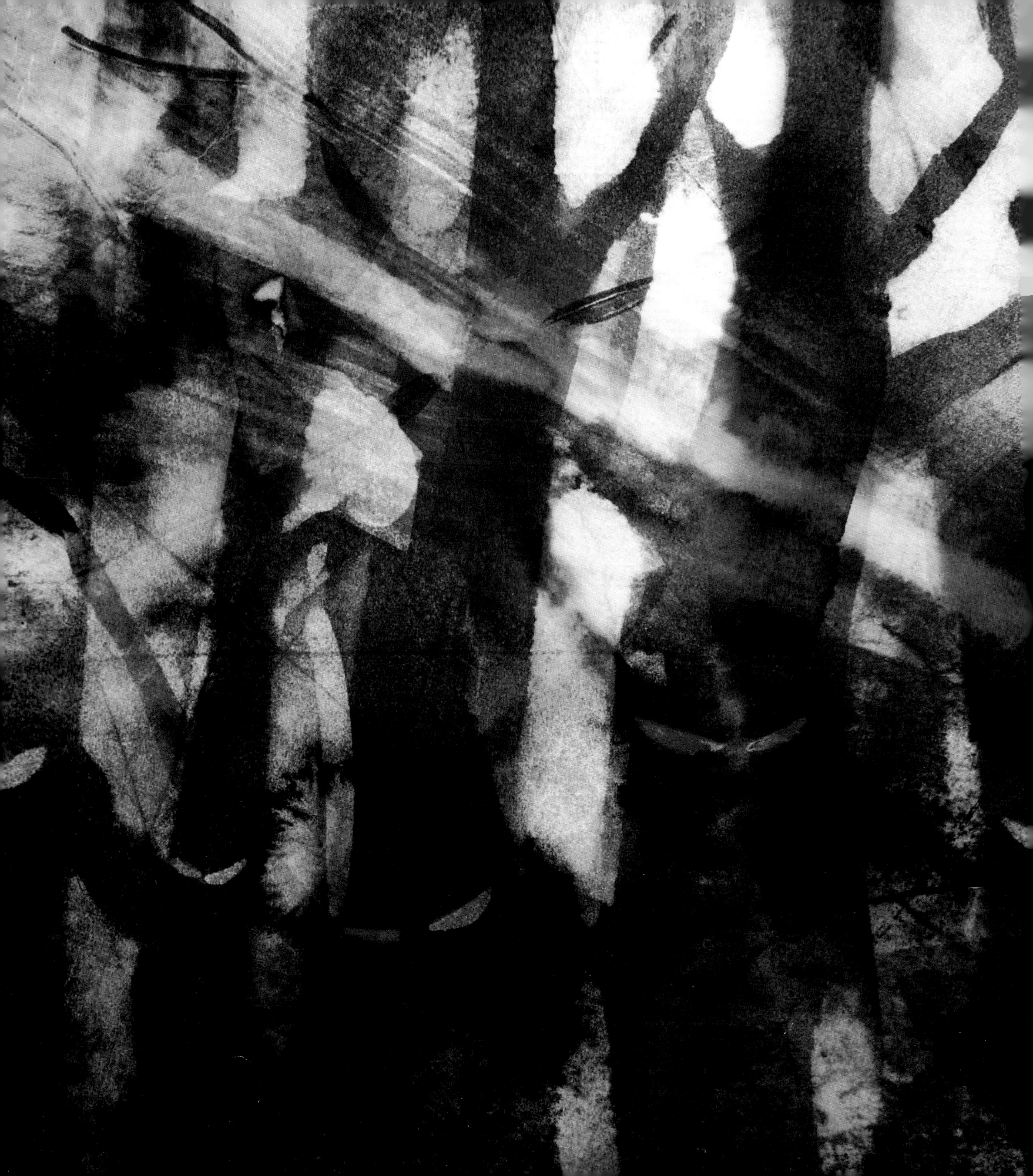